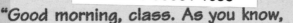
"Good morning, class. As you know, we have our test today."

Mrs.   classroom, copies of the math test under her arm. Although Sabrina had tried to study the night before, she just hadn't been able to concentrate, especially after Salem started mewling in his sleep. So now she was cramming.

"I hope you all studied, because the test is a thorough one, though I don't think it's too hard, really." Mrs. Quick paused as a warm wind blew through the room, flinging a few papers off her desk.

Sabrina knew that the strange breeze was the magical Fair Wind she had brewed up. She crossed her fingers and hoped, *Maybe she'll call the test off because it's unfair.*

"Well, anyway," said Mrs. Quick, "I was saying that this shouldn't be too hard for any of you. But just to be fair, I'm going to make it an open-book test."

The students cheered.

"But only for the dumb students," Mrs. Quick continued. "They need all the help they can get. Smart students like Sabrina Spellman should be able to ace this test without their books."

"What?" cried Sabrina. "Wait a minute—"

Okay, maybe not everything *is better when it's fair,* she thought.

Sabrina, the Teenage Witch™ books

Available from ARCHWAY Paperbacks

Sabrina The Teenage Witch™

Prom Time

Bobby JG Weiss and David Cody Weiss

Based on Characters Appearing in Archie Comics

And based upon the television series
Sabrina, The Teenage Witch
Created for television by Nell Scovell
Developed for television by Jonathan Schmock

AN ARCHWAY PAPERBACK
Published by POCKET BOOKS
New York London Toronto Sydney Tokyo Singapore

AN ARCHWAY PAPERBACK *Original*

An Archway Paperback published by
POCKET BOOKS, a division of Simon & Schuster Inc.
1230 Avenue of the Americas, New York, NY 10020

ISBN: 0-671-02816-2

First Archway Paperback printing April 1999

10 9 8 7 6 5 4 3 2 1

AN ARCHWAY PAPERBACK and colophon are
registered trademarks of Simon & Schuster Inc.

SABRINA THE TEENAGE WITCH and all related titles, logos
and characters are trademarks of Archie Comics Publications, Inc.

Printed in the U.S.A.

IL: 4+

To Sissa Betta,
whose prom picture will forever be the envy of us all

Prom Time

☆

Chapter 1

☆

It's not fair!"

A frowning Sabrina Spellman banged her way into her house, slammed the front door behind her, tossed her book bag down, and stomped all the way into the kitchen.

Nobody was there.

That made her anger jump up another notch. How could she whine and look for sympathy if nobody was around? "It's not fair!" she shouted at the empty room, hitting her fist on the counter for good measure. "Ouch!" Sucking the side of her hand, she jerked open the freezer door, intent on drowning her sorrows in a big bowl of pistachio butterscotch ice cream. Just then her aunt Zelda entered.

"Do I detect a temper tantrum in progress?" Zelda asked sweetly.

In reply, Sabrina jabbed her right index finger skyward. A crack of angry thunder shook the house.

Zelda remained perfectly calm. "I'll take that as a yes."

"There is no justice in the world," Sabrina stated, and as if that explained everything, she dug her spoon deep into the half gallon of ice cream, loaded it up, and crammed it into her mouth.

Zelda folded her arms. "You know, bowls are a wonderful invention. For one thing, they keep you from wearing your food on your clothes."

Sabrina looked down to find a gob of ice cream on her favorite sweater. With an incoherent growl she zapped the stain away, then magically jammed the entire half gallon of ice cream into a dish. Hugging the huge overflowing bowl possessively, she carried it to the kitchen table, sat down, and started hacking away with her spoon again.

Zelda settled into the chair next to her fuming niece. "On a scale of one to ten, I'd say this must be an eleven. What's wrong, sweetheart?"

"Nothing that moving to another school district couldn't cure. Oh, Aunt Zelda, it's just—"

"Not fair!" finished Sabrina's aunt Hilda, stomping into the kitchen.

Sabrina glared at her. "Hey, you stole my line."

"Tough. You don't own it."

"But I said it first!"

2

"Too bad! I said it with more feeling!"

"Hey, hey, hey!" Zelda jumped to her feet and stretched her arms out like a referee ready to keep two boxers from lunging at each other. "What is going on here? You're both acting like three-year-olds."

"It's all Libby's fault," sulked Sabrina. "I'm so sick of her sometimes I could just . . . just . . . *spit!*" But instead of spitting she wolfed down another spoonful of ice cream.

"Spit?" Hilda laughed in mock amusement. "Spit? Go ahead, spit all you want. All you'll lose is a little body moisture and dignity. I mean, it's not like losing your *freedom.*"

Zelda eyed her sister. "And what's that supposed to mean?"

"It means," said Hilda, plopping down in a chair, "that if Antonio Banderas called me up and begged me to go out on a date, I'd have to say no. It means"—and she zapped a spoon into her hand—"that if I won a free trip to Tahiti, I'd have to turn it down. It means"—she dug into Sabrina's ice cream with the spoon—"that my life is ruined!"

Despite her frustration, Sabrina was curious. "How has your life been ruined?"

Hilda uttered a little moan. "I've been grounded."

"You mean, like, you-can't-leave-the-house grounded?"

Hilda nodded. "For a whole week!"

Now Zelda understood. Her eyes widened as she murmured, "Ohhhhhh," and sympathetically patted her sister's shoulder.

"I don't get it," Sabrina said. "Who grounded you, the Witches' Council?"

Hilda gave a sour laugh. "If only."

"No, Sabrina," said Zelda, "this is worse."

As far as Sabrina knew, nothing could be worse than being in trouble with the Witches' Council. "Who, then?"

"Daddy!" blurted Hilda.

Rubbing Hilda's shoulders in an attempt to calm her, Zelda explained, "It's a punishment our father put on Hilda centuries ago"—her voice lowered—"that she elected to put off till later."

Hilda's cheeks flashed red. "Oh, fine. First you're sympathetic, now you turn on me."

"I'm not turning on you. I'm just telling Sabrina the truth. If you'd had the courage to take your punishment five hundred years ago, you wouldn't be in this position today."

"If I'd had that kind of courage five hundred years ago, I wouldn't have gotten into this predicament in the first place."

"You have only yourself to blame."

Hilda turned to Sabrina. "Don't you just hate it when she gets sanctimonious?"

"All I'm saying," said Zelda, "is that you have to take your punishment whether you want to or not, and it's unfair of you to make me listen to you complain about it. The last time you complained so much, I ended up wearing earplugs for a full week."

"And you deserved it when they got stuck in your ears. Snitch."

Zelda reacted to Hilda's last word as if it were a physical slap. "What did you call me?"

"Snitch," Hilda repeated. "You told Daddy on me. That's how he found out, isn't it?"

"It is not," said Zelda, insulted. "I was helping to clean up, just as you asked me to."

"I never asked you to clean up!"

"Yes, you did. You don't think all those turkey feathers picked themselves up, do you?"

Now it was Sabrina's turn to play referee and keep her aunts from lunging at each other. "Time out!" she ordered. "Does anybody want to tell me what you're talking—I'm sorry, what you're *yelling*—about?"

"Only the dumbest thing in the world," Hilda said, "and it wasn't even my fault. If only I hadn't gone to that dance with Drell . . ."

Sabrina dropped her spoon. "This is about a dance? My problem is about a dance, too—specifically my prom."

Hilda's instant smile was too big to be genuine. Clearly she was anxious to turn the conversation away from herself. "Oh, do tell us what's wrong, Sabrina. We'd love to help."

Zelda glared at her sister as she added, "And one of us actually means it."

"Well . . ." Now that she had their attention,

Sabrina didn't know how to explain the day's events without sounding like a whiny baby. "The spring prom is coming up, and Libby Chessler is taking over the whole event. I just found out today that she and the other cheerleaders have been in charge of planning it for weeks. Mr. Kraft appointed them, and none of them told the rest of us. Now the dance is a week away, and nobody's had any input except Libby and her zombie girls. They're claiming that it's too late to bring in anybody new to help them."

"Really?" Hilda's expression of concern was genuine now. "That really *is* unfair. Of course, you could always turn them into goats and take over the committee yourself."

Sabrina grinned. "That's not a bad idea."

"Don't you dare," Zelda warned. Turning to Hilda, she added, "Enough about turning dance committee members into animals. Why do you think you got grounded in the first place?"

"But I didn't do it!" Hilda insisted. When Zelda's expression didn't change, Hilda simply turned back to Sabrina's ice cream.

"Wait a minute," Sabrina said, stopping a heaping spoonful halfway to Hilda's mouth. "How can you be grounded now for something you did centuries ago? Isn't that going a little overboard on the whole discipline thing?"

Hilda just grunted and rerouted her spoon around Sabrina's hand and into her mouth.

"She's grounded *now*," Zelda explained, "because she didn't want to be grounded for a whole year back *then*. She sweet-talked our father into letting her serve one week at a time, once per decade. That way the punishment would get spread out over five hundred and twenty years and wouldn't be so hard to endure."

"Unfortunately," said Hilda through a mouthful of frozen goo, *"which* week per decade I get grounded is picked with a randomizer spell, so I can't schedule around it. I'm always caught by surprise."

"Which is only fair," Zelda said. "Otherwise, it wouldn't be much of a punishment, would it?" An expression of alarm suddenly darkened her features. "Wait a minute—this is 1999, the year before the millennium. Isn't this the balloon decade?"

"Balloon decade?" Sabrina repeated, clueless.

Hilda let out a heartbreaking moan. "Ohhhh, that's right!" She buried her face in her hands and sobbed. "I'm not grounded for *one* week, I'm grounded for *two!*"

Zelda looked guilty, explaining to Sabrina, "It's like some home mortgages that have a big balloon payment at the end. Our father arranged this punishment to end with a double grounding—two weeks."

"Talk about ending a punishment with a bang," Hilda sobbed.

Sabrina tried to sympathize with her aunt, but her own misery overwhelmed all other feelings. "I'm sorry, Aunt Hilda, but at least you don't have to put up with Libby," she said. "I mean, what am I going to do? If Libby organizes the prom, the cheerleaders and the jocks will have a private hall with a rockin' disc jockey and really good food, and the rest of us will eat packaged cookies, drink watered-down punch, and dance to old disco music in a closet." Sabrina aimed her spoon for more ice cream, but Zelda gracefully snatched up the bowl and carried it to the counter.

"That's enough sugar. It's almost time for dinner."

"But I hardly had any yet," Sabrina said.

"See?" said Hilda, poised to wolf down the last big spoonful she'd managed to snag. "She likes to spoil everything."

"Did somebody just say 'spoil'?" came a deep voice from the stairway. A sleek black American shorthair cat padded down the last few steps and plodded into the kitchen. "That seems to be the word of the day. My mood's been spoiled, my afternoon's been spoiled, and my parole hearing's been spoiled, all in one fell swoop."

"Is it safe to ask what happened?" Sabrina asked as the cat leaped up to the countertop.

Salem hung his head. "I just got a letter from the Other Realm Parole Board. Seems they found out I've still got a subscription to *World Conquest*

8

Monthly. I tell ya, it's just not fair. They snoop into everything I do!"

"I thought that was what being on parole was all about," Sabrina noted.

"Salem, you told me you canceled your subscription to that magazine months ago." Zelda wasn't sympathetic now; she was angry. "You know it's a condition of your parole that you avoid all literature involving subjugation of any kind."

Salem turned to Sabrina. "Sub-what?"

"You're not supposed to read about anybody taking over anybody else."

"Oh." Salem turned back to Zelda. "Well, I couldn't help it. Their articles are engrossing, their research is impeccable, and besides, their centerfold photos are the best. Last month's picture of Saddam Hussein kissing a baby camel was worthy of framing."

"So let me guess," said Hilda. "You got grounded."

Salem gave her a funny look. "Grounded? What would be so awful about staying home and napping all day? No, I get to do extra community service." His ears flattened against his furry skull. "I hate community service!"

Sabrina remembered her own stint at community service several months earlier. She'd ended up working in a rumor mill, but she had had other choices, most of them rather gross. "Washing old witches isn't too hard," she told Salem.

He shuddered at the thought. "Please. It's bad enough I have to wash myself with my own tongue."

"Yeah, and with your fish breath, every time you open your mouth for a bath we have to use extra air freshener," Hilda muttered.

Salem frowned—not easy for a feline. "The next time you fall asleep, just know that I'll be hovering over you, breathing heavily."

"All right, everybody, get a grip." Zelda looked each of them in the eye, one by one. "This has gone far enough. We all have problems, but we have to deal with them whether we think they're fair or not. Hilda, by your own arrangement you're stuck in this house for two weeks, so why don't you make the best of it? Salem, you knew you weren't supposed to read that magazine, so why don't you just contact the Other Realm Community Service Appointment Bureau and get it over with? And, Sabrina, you have to learn to deal with people like Libby, though I advise you to do so the mortal way. Hilda is living proof that magic can be more of a problem than a solution."

Hilda started to reply, but Salem interrupted her. "That's a mighty fine speech, Zelda, but it's easy to lecture when you don't have any problems of your own."

"Oh, but I do have problems," Zelda assured him with a smile. "I have to put up with the three of you." And with that, she left the room.

Salem's lower lip trembled. "I feel so rejected."

"I think we ought to put a spell on her magic mirror so that the next time she looks into it, it cracks," Hilda grumped.

Sabrina only stared down at her shoes, feeling a little guilty. "She's right, you know. All we do is sit around and complain."

"My favorite pastime," said Salem.

"Second to eating, that is," Hilda added.

"Oh, come on, you guys." Sabrina got to her feet and forced herself to stand tall. "So we've got problems—big deal. We'll solve them. After all, when the going gets tough, the tough get going, right?" She paused. *"Right?"*

Salem gave in. "Okay, okay, I agree. Whoever said life was a bowl of cherries obviously never ate fruit. Or are cherries a vegetable?"

"All right, I'll stop complaining, too," Hilda said. "When the world throws us lemons, we'll make lemonade, blah-blah-blah."

"Great!" Sabrina smiled at her aunt and the cat. "See, we're feeling better already, right?"

"Right!"

Then they looked at each other and whined at once, "But it's still not fair!"

Chapter 2

☆

Sabrina made plans.

At school the next day before classes started, she hurried to the office of Willard H. Kraft, vice-principal of Westbridge High School. Kraft could not have been described as a loving man, nor did he possess a strong sense of fairness, but theoretically, he could be persuaded to see reason.

She tapped on his closed office door. "Mr. Kraft?"

"I'm not in yet," a voice said behind her.

Sabrina squealed in surprise and whirled around to find Kraft standing behind her, his briefcase in his hand. "Oh, Mr. Kraft! There you are!"

"Yes, here I am," Kraft agreed, giving her a thin smile. "And there you are, blocking my door."

"Oh. Sorry." Sabrina stepped aside so that he

could jab his key in the lock. "Mr. Kraft, can I talk to you for a minute?"

He pushed his door open and stepped inside. "Miss Spellman, whatever the question is, I'm sure the answer is no."

Sabrina made herself chuckle. Kraft wasn't making a joke—he was being serious—and she had learned long ago that laughing was the only safe way to respond. "Ha-ha, good one! No, really, I need to talk to you about something important."

Kraft sighed. "All right, out with it. But be quick." After striding to his desk, he opened his briefcase and started shuffling papers around.

"It's about the spring prom," Sabrina said, following him inside. "See, I was thinking maybe it would be a good thing if all the different social strata of the school population be represented at planning meetings—"

Kraft lifted his head from his paper shuffling. "I beg your pardon? Did I just hear you say 'social strata'?"

"Yeah, you know—like the nerds, the partyers, the jocks, and the jockettes."

"I know what the term means, Miss Spellman. I'm just surprised to hear it issue forth from the mouth of a high school student. Most teenage conversations I overhear are composed of mono-syllabic words and animal grunts, so naturally I assumed that was the extent of your communication skills."

Sabrina took a step backward. "Okay, maybe

this isn't the best time to talk about this. I'll come back when you're in a better mood.'"

"That's unlikely ever to happen as long as I have this job," Kraft snapped, "so let me just say this: you're concerned that Libby is in charge of the Prom Planning Committee, am I right?"

Sabrina nodded. "Bingo."

"And you want to be on the committee, but she won't let you. Right?"

"Wow, bingo again, Mr. Kraft. You're on a winning streak." She tried a friendly grin.

He frowned. "Don't try to butter me up."

Sabrina wiped the grin off her face, wondering if Kraft had owned a puppy as a kid and, if so, had the puppy liked him?

"Let me put it this way," Kraft told her. "I've survived high school administration long enough to appreciate having a major school event in good hands. Miss Chessler is an excellent organizer, and she's proven time and again that she can motivate students to perform boring, repetitive, even excruciating physical labor for free. That's what the Prom Planning Committee needs, and that's what it has in Libby Chessler. End of discussion."

"But, Mr. Kraft, it also needs equal representation for all students," Sabrina pressed. "As it is, only the popular kids will be represented."

Kraft renewed his tight smile. "Then it will be a very popular prom. Now excuse me, I have a boring meeting to attend." The bell rang. "And you have an equally boring class to get to."

Sabrina exited Kraft's office, fuming, but she wasn't about to give up. "Okay, if he won't help, I'll try talking to Libby again." That made her laugh out loud, but the challenge didn't dampen her determination. "Miracles can happen," she kept telling herself. "Bumblebees fly, which should be aerodynamically impossible, so maybe I can pull off a miracle today, too."

Between English and history, Sabrina intercepted Libby in the hallway.

"Eww," Libby greeted her.

"Hi," Sabrina said. "Look, Libby, can we talk about the Prom Planning Committee? I really want to—"

"Isn't it amazing," Libby said loudly to her cheerleader friends, "how freaks never seem to hear the word 'no'?" She faced Sabrina head-on. "I said no before, and I meant it."

"I'm sure you did," said Sabrina, gathering her pride around her while preparing to stomp all over it in the name of progress, "but have you really considered all the work this is going to involve? I mean, there must be something we non-cheerleader types can do"—*stomp stomp!*— "to make your life easier and more pleasant."

Libby smirked. "Of course there is. You could vanish into thin air and take the geeks with you." She and her cohorts enjoyed a loud laugh and walked away.

"Yeah, and wouldn't you wig out if I actually did it?" Sabrina muttered, her index finger twitching.

So much for "mortal solutions." By the end of the day, Sabrina was so mad at the injustice of it all that she actually yelled at Harvey Kinkle. "Hi, Sabrina," he greeted, sauntering up to her locker after the final bell.

"What!" she barked.

Harvey shied away from her. "Whoa, what's with you?"

"Oh, Harvey, I'm sorry." Sabrina slumped against her locker. "This whole Prom Planning Committee thing's got me worked up, that's all."

"Like me and the wrestling thing," Harvey said. "I tried so hard to get on the wrestling team, but I didn't make it."

"I'm sorry, Harvey."

"It's okay. I'm bummed, but not bummed enough not to share some bummed feelings for your prom committee thing."

Sabrina felt a little tingle in her chest. She felt it every time Harvey said something cute like that . . . even if he did say it in a strangely roundabout way. "Thanks, but I don't think bummed feelings will be enough to overcome Libby's over-inflated ego."

"No, I guess not." Harvey's expression brightened. "What about getting bummed together over a couple of sodas at the Slicery?"

"I'd love to," said Sabrina, "but one of my

aunts is grounded, and I promised to go right home and play Monopoly with her." Only after she said that did she realize how bizarre it sounded.

Before Harvey could comment, Valerie Birkhead appeared—or rather she slogged her way up to Sabrina's locker, radiating so much depression that Sabrina could almost feel the air molecules drooping around her. "Hi, Harvey," Valerie said in a dead monotone. "Hi, Sabrina. Do you think anybody would notice if I just crawled into my locker and stayed there for the rest of my life?"

Great, more trouble, Sabrina thought. "Val, what happened?"

"I just talked to Libby to see if she'd let me on the Prom Planning Committee."

"Let me guess—she said no?"

"She told me she didn't have time to reject me personally, but if I talked to you, you could pass on the same rejection speech she gave you earlier."

"Gee, and I forgot to take notes."

Valerie sniffled. "She also wondered why I wanted to be on the committee since I obviously won't have a date for the prom. I lied and told her I was going with Todd Earling. Now what am I going to do?"

"Todd's a nice guy. Ask him to go," Harvey suggested.

"Oh, right," Valerie said, "like I don't face enough rejection in my life."

Sabrina slammed her locker shut. "Ooo, this has gone too far! I wish I could just zap Libby!"

"Zap?" Harvey asked. "Like with lightning?"

Flashing an evil grin, Sabrina said, "Something like that. Look, Valerie, don't let Libby get to you. We'll figure something out, and somehow we'll get you to the prom with Todd. But right now I gotta go."

"Her aunt's been grounded and they have to play Monopoly," Harvey explained helpfully.

"Don't ask," Sabrina told Valerie. "I'll see you tomorrow, okay?"

"Sure," Valerie moaned. "Maybe we can arrange to get rejected for something even on Saturday."

By the time she got home, Sabrina was furious and depressed at the same time—a weird combination that made her want to beat up a pillow, but very slowly. "Mortal solutions do *not* work with Libby," she told her aunts, "because Libby is not a person. She's a bad dream with legs."

Hilda was already setting up the Monopoly board on the kitchen table. "Sabrina, why are you letting her get to you like this? You've dealt successfully with Libby before."

"And you've done it without using magic," added Zelda as she made tea.

They were right. Sabrina had once persuaded Libby to cover for her when the members of Sabrina's magically talented rock band lost their talent, and she'd even learned to sympathize with Libby's softer aspects once when she accidentally turned the cheerleader into a life-size puzzle. "But this situation is completely different" was all she could think of to say.

"Different?" asked Zelda, carrying three cups of tea to the table. "How?"

"Well, it's . . . it's . . ." Sabrina flailed her arms. "This is happening *now*, and all the other problems happened *then*. Isn't that enough?" She grabbed the dice and tossed to see who would start the game. She rolled a two. *That figures,* she thought sourly.

Hilda picked up the dice. "Sounds to me as if somebody refuses to bend a little."

"Yeah—Libby."

"No," said Zelda, "you."

"But she's not being fair," Sabrina said.

Hilda held up her hand in the signal to stop. She rolled the dice and got a five. "Enough with the fair-unfair speeches, Sabrina. Didn't you learn anything from my older and wiser sister yesterday? We all have to deal with problems."

Zelda regarded her younger sister in awe. "Why, Hilda, I never thought I'd hear you say something so supportive about my advice."

Hilda beamed sincerity. "Zelda, sometimes you're advice is so stunningly accurate, I *can't* take it because it would be too good for me. Now can I have the horsie marker?"

Zelda snatched up the horsie marker. "I see, you're just trying to butter me up. Well, forget it. I get the horsie. You can have the top hat."

"But I don't want the top hat!"

Sabrina sat down and placed her ocean liner marker on the starting square. "Excuse me, but can we just play? I've got enough arguments running in my head as it is. Who's banker?"

"I am," said Hilda as she reached for the little trays of fake money. "If I have to be grounded and horseless, I get the money."

Sabrina had a hard time concentrating, especially when Salem joined them and started giving everyone strategy tips. "No, no, no, don't use your Get Out of Jail Free card now," he advised her at one point. "There might come a time when you've got no cash and you end up behind bars. Then the card is a real life saver." He sighed. "If only I'd had one when Drell caught me trying to take over the world."

"Can I use magic?" Sabrina asked.

"To get out of jail free?" asked Hilda. "Of course not."

"No, with Libby."

"Sabrina." Zelda stopped the game with a look. "Sweetie, haven't you learned by now? Fairness and equality are issues in both realms, and magic can't solve the problems they cause."

"On the other hand, there's nothing wrong with fighting fire with fire," Hilda pointed out. "You

know my motto—if you can't join 'em, beat 'em."
As she said this, a huge mallet appeared in her
hands. "What works for Bugs Bunny can work for
you."

Sabrina laughed and reached for the mallet
when a sound like *ka-PONK!* made her jump.
Something popped out of the toaster.

"It's a message from the Other Realm," said
Zelda, picking it up. She held it out to Sabrina.
"And it's for you."

Sabrina took the little white envelope. The first
thing she noticed was the smell. The paper reeked
of perfume, and the scent seemed to be a combination of roses and . . . butterscotch?

Hilda sniffed. "Uh-oh."

Zelda sniffed. "Oh, dear."

"What?" Sabrina asked, afraid to open it now.
But her curiosity was too great. Gingerly she lifted
the triangular flap.

A brightly colored greeting card zipped out and,
floating open by itself, issued its message in a
vaguely familiar voice. "Sabrina darling, how are
you? I just heard the news, and I must tell you, I
am simply ecstatic! This is the most wonderful
time of your life, so you need to plan everything
perfectly. Naturally that will require my expertise,
so I'll be stopping by soon. Ta till then!" The
greeting card closed itself and slipped back into its
envelope.

Sabrina looked at the flowery handwriting on
the envelope.

Sabrina Spellman
Toaster 47882
The Mortal Realm

A combination of delight and apprehension crept over Sabrina. "Does that voice belong to who I think it belongs to?" she asked her aunts.

They nodded. "It looks like your aunt Vesta is coming to help you get ready for the prom."

Chapter 3

Actually, a visit from Vesta wasn't a bad thing. Sabrina liked her eldest aunt. The problem was that Vesta lived for style, and what she considered stylish wasn't necessarily in tune with the rest of the universe. As for her personality, Zelda once described it as "somewhat forceful." All that, combined with stunning good looks, an ego the size of Nebraska, and powerful witch magic, made Vesta a little hard to take.

On the other hand, Sabrina appreciated her eldest aunt's advance notice. When dealing with witch relatives, advance notice of anything was unusual. More often than not, Other Realm visitors just marched in through the linen closet whenever they pleased and asked what was for dinner. At least this time Sabrina could prepare for Vesta's visit.

And she had all of three minutes to do it.

A puff of smoke and a jingle of gold jewelry, and Aunt Vesta suddenly stood in the kitchen. "Zelda! Hilda! And my dear Sabrina. Did you get my card?" she asked, flashing her perfectly white teeth in a perfectly radiant smile.

Sabrina held the greeting card up. "Yeah, three minutes ago."

"Perfect! I didn't want to just pop in unannounced." Vesta tried to give Sabrina a hug, but the minute she reached out, she almost fell over. "Oops," she said with a merry chuckle. "Silly me. These things are harder to walk in than six-inch stilettos."

Sabrina looked down to see that Vesta's feet were encased in figure skates. In fact, Vesta was decked out from head to toe in a sparkling ice-skating costume that was so tight she must have been poured into it. Not that she didn't look good. Aunt Vesta's curvy figure was the envy of—well, just about every woman who saw her, mortal or witch. But no amount of style could help a person walk in ice skates across a linoleum floor. "Give Auntie Vesta a hug," she ended up saying, holding out her arms but not moving any more of her body than that.

Sabrina obligingly gave Vesta a hug, and Vesta gave her two enthusiastic "social kisses," or what Valerie referred to as "elitist air smacks." Sabrina thought it was silly to kiss the air near a person's

24

ear, but it was one of those annoying little social procedures that some people took seriously. Vesta certainly did.

Then Vesta held Sabrina by the shoulders and looked her up and down as if evaluating every inch of her . . . which was exactly what she was doing. "Oh, you're growing up so fast," she said admiringly. "Already it's time for your first prom! Personally, I can't wait. It's a week from tomorrow—next Saturday night, right?"

"Uh, yeah," said Sabrina. She wanted to add, "And you're not invited," but instead she asked, "How did you find out?"

"Darling, I know the major events in everyone's life. I am your auntie Vesta, after all."

"What she means," said Hilda, not hiding her irritation, "is that she's got one of those big Witchworks Social Calendar Systems that keeps track of every aspect of her life . . . and everyone else's, too."

"It's so complex that her Other Realm computer has to run off its own magical power generator," Zelda added, not without envy.

"Which needs to be replaced," Vesta told her. "It must be wearing out because I actually missed a hair appointment yesterday. Can you imagine? I had to coif myself!" She kissed her pointing finger. "How fortunate that I'm as talented as I am beautiful!" She flashed her smile again. "But enough of that. I just wanted to pop in and make sure everything's running smoothly so far. No glitches in the dress plans? Dinner reservations made at the finest restaurant?" She gazed into Sabrina's eyes as if trying to see into her very soul. "I presume you *do* have a date."

"Yes, I have a date," Sabrina answered, amused despite herself. Vesta was a busybody, but her interest was so genuine it was hard for Sabrina to be mad. "His name is Harvey Kinkle."

Vesta squinched up her nose as if a bad smell had wafted by. "Mortals and their ridiculous names. Ah, well. What's his cute factor?"

"Ten out of ten," Sabrina assured her.

"Then he'll do." Vesta raised her finger. "Well, I must be going. My party is still in progress, but I just couldn't wait to congratulate you, Sabrina." In a confidential whisper she added, "I've rented the entire island of Greenland for a Winter Paradise party. Isn't that a riot?" With a wave of her hand, she disappeared in a shower of sparkles, the colors of which matched her outfit, of course. "I'll be back soon! Ta till then!" her voice called out after she was gone.

Hilda waved at the empty air. "Hasta la Vesta, baby."

Sabrina regarded her aunts. "Why don't you guys like Vesta?"

"It's not that we don't like her, Sabrina," Zelda began.

"It's just that she drives us crazy," Hilda finished. "Always the pretty one."

"Always the perfect one."

"Always the one with her nose in everybody's business."

Hilda and Zelda glared at each other. "She definitely has all the fun."

The weekend passed, and with every moment of it, Sabrina got more and more nervous. What had Vesta meant when she said, "Personally, I can't wait"? Just how much did she intend to interfere?

Sabrina already knew enough about the eldest Spellman sister to realize she couldn't stop Vesta from giving advice. Convinced of her superior tastes, Vesta could make herself impossible to ignore. "But I could handle some hair and make-up tips," she confided to Salem. "The problem is, Aunt Vesta acted like she intended to go to the prom with me. You don't think she . . . ?"

"Vesta looks incredible for somebody over eight hundred years old," Salem answered, "but even she wouldn't try to crash a high school prom." Salem paused. "But don't quote me on that."

"Thanks, cat. I feel so much better."

Hilda didn't help the situation either. Being grounded could be aggravating for a teenager, but for a grown witch who normally could zap herself from Shanghai to Seattle on a whim, it was pure torture. Hilda tried to be cheerful, but by Saturday she was sprawled on the couch staring at the

TV and eating everything in sight. By Sunday she not only had a horrible stomachache but she had also developed the tendency to moan instead of talk.

By Monday morning she was pressed against the glass-paneled kitchen door, staring outside with wide, glazed eyes like a bug trapped in a jar. After getting ready for school, Sabrina trotted downstairs for breakfast and noticed this unusual display. "Aunt Hilda, are you all right?"

Hilda only grunted.

Sabrina turned to Zelda, who was cooking eggs. "Aunt Zelda, is this normal?"

"For Hilda, yes," Zelda confessed. "She doesn't deal well with being grounded."

"But why is she staring out at the back patio?"

Salem, who was sitting on the kitchen table, offered, "It's the next best thing to being there?"

Sabrina wished she could keep her poor aunt company, but she had to go to school—not that she really wanted to, but today was a big meeting of the Prom Planning Committee. One way or another, Sabrina intended to be at it.

After a hasty breakfast and a bumpy bus trip, she rushed through the halls of Westbridge High School, heading for her least favorite place: the office of the vice-principal.

"Oh, not you again," Mr. Kraft said as she walked in.

Hearing that from any other person, Sabrina

would have been horribly insulted. But from Mr. Kraft, it was a standard greeting. "Mr. Kraft, can I talk to you?"

"You just did. Good-bye." He turned back to the stack of papers in his hand.

Sabrina wasn't going to let him off the hook this time. "Mr. Kraft, I demand to be on the Prom Planning Committee. There's only one week left. At this point I couldn't possibly disrupt any special plans Libby's made for the popular kids, right?"

Slowly setting his papers down, Kraft lifted his eyes until he was looking at her even though his head was still bowed. The posture made him look like a cheap horror-thriller bad guy. "You *demand?*" he said in a low voice.

Sabrina gulped. "Uh, I mean . . . pretty please?"

"Oh, all right—"

"Wow, thank you!"

"I'm not through yet."

"Sorry." Sabrina tried to stifle her whoops of triumph.

"I was about to say all right, you can attend one meeting," said Kraft, "but only one. I'll tell Libby that today's meeting must be public. All those students who wish to attend can do so and hear what plans have been made. However"— and he emphasized the word—"you will be a spectator only. You may ask questions, but Libby is in charge of the proceedings. Is that acceptable?"

It wasn't what Sabrina had hoped for, but clearly she wasn't going to get anything better. "Okay," she agreed. "Thank you, Mr. Kraft."

"You're welcome. Now do me a favor in return."

"Sure thing."

"Leave."

Sabrina left.

For a Monday morning, Sabrina's classes moved along pleasantly enough. By lunchtime she was in a good mood and looking forward to crashing Libby's meeting after school. Most of all, she enjoyed Libby's lunchtime announcement about it. "Excuse me, everybody," Libby said imperiously. Nobody heard her.

Sabrina, Valerie, and Harvey were sitting at their usual table, which meant that Libby was all of three feet away. Sabrina couldn't resist helping out. "Hey, everybody," she called, standing up. "Libby has something important to say!"

Libby glared daggers at her. "I can do my own shutting up, thank you very much."

"Really? I hadn't noticed." Then Sabrina feigned shock. "Oh, I'm sorry. You were going to say something?"

With a toss of her head, Libby announced, "As head of the Prom Planning Committee, I've decided to hold an open meeting after school today. Anyone wishing to come can sit in a special roped-off area and listen while the committee members discuss their plans."

"What an excellent idea," Sabrina said loudly. "Can we ask questions?"

Valerie, who always preferred to keep a low profile, grabbed Sabrina's arm and whispered, "Why are you antagonizing her?"

"Because I can?" Sabrina merrily suggested.

Libby overheard. "Sorry, but I don't antagonize that easily," she said primly. "Yes, anybody can ask questions."

"Whether we receive an answer is another matter," Sabrina muttered.

Libby heard that remark, too, but only pursed her lips in response. "The meeting will start at three o'clock sharp," she said. To Sabrina she added, "That means the little hand will be on the three and the big hand will be on the twelve."

"Wow," Sabrina said to Harvey. "And I thought she could only read digital clocks."

Harvey snickered. Libby scowled.

The rest of the day passed quickly, and in no time classes were over. At ten minutes to three, Sabrina hurried to the bathroom. It was one thing to take Libby on head-to-head; it was another to do it with messy hair.

But when Sabrina pushed on the bathroom door, it pushed back. Then it opened a crack and Cee Cee, one of Libby's cheerleader cronies, peered through. "Private meeting," she said. "Use the other bathroom." And she closed the door again.

Sabrina stood there for a moment, wondering. *Private meeting? Could it be Libby's having a meeting* before *the meeting?* If only she could be a fly on the wall . . .

Then Sabrina looked at her index finger. *Why not?* she thought.

Chapter 4

☆

Only after Sabrina had turned herself into a fly and crawled under the bathroom door did she realize that flies and bathrooms were a gross combination. *Oh, well,* she thought, *I'm not that kind of fly.*

Sure enough, Libby was there, surrounded by the rest of the cheerleaders—or rather, the Prom Planning Committee. "Who was at the door?" Libby asked Cee Cee.

"Spellman," replied Cee Cee. "I told her to buzz off."

Buzz off? As in fly? Sabrina tried to laugh, only to discover that flies can't laugh. Instead, her long proboscis curled and uncurled rapidly three times, and her wings twitched, making a soft crinkly sound. An overwhelming urge to rub her antennae made her forget that she was still on the floor—an easy target for the sole of a cheerleader's shoe. When Libby said, "You'd better stand freak watch at the door," and Cee Cee moved to obey, Sabrina realized her danger. With a loud buzzing sound, she sprang into the air.

Cee Cee waved her hand in front of her face. "Eww! Flies in the bathroom!"

Sabrina buzzed around her nose for a few more seconds, then zipped over to the wall, far out of reach, to get her bearings. It wasn't easy keeping her stubby fly body in control, and looking out through multifaceted eyes didn't help. To Sabrina, the bathroom was filled with about twenty Libbys and an equal number of Cee Cees and Jills and other cheerleaders. *What a nightmare,* Sabrina thought. *No wonder flies are so paranoid.* On the other hand, being able to walk up a wall wasn't bad. Without any conscious effort on her part, Sabrina felt her tiny fly feet simply stick wherever she put them, but she could lift them whenever she wanted to. *Definitely cool,* she thought. *Spider-Man, eat your heart out.*

"Okay, listen up," Libby said to her committee members. "I need your reports quickly. Theme."

Jill spoke up. "The Camelot theme is coming along well. You, of course, will be Guinevere, queen of the prom, but I don't think we'll be able to use real swords in the duel."

Swords? Duel? Sabrina thought in alarm.

"If Allen and Darryl are going to fight for the

right to be crowned king, we need weapons," Libby snapped.

Jill just shrugged. "Mr. Kraft won't allow anything lethal."

Libby gave in, obviously angry. "All right, buy two fake swords, then. And schedule a time when I can try on my crown to make sure it fits. Now what about decorations?"

"I need more help," Jill said reluctantly.

"Then name some assistants at three o'clock," ordered Libby. "Just be sure you don't use geeks. They're so uncoordinated they're worthless. The decorations have to be perfect, got it? I want this to be the spring prom that everybody remembers me by." Libby turned to Cheri, the ditziest girl in the school. "How's the dance floor coming?"

"Wow, okay, like, my dad designed a wooden overlay that we can, like, put in the gym?" Cheri said, making her statement sound more like a question. "It'll be painted to look, you know, like the Round Table?"

"And the dance zones?"

Sabrina absently rubbed her bulbous head with a long, hairy leg. *Dance zones?* she wondered, her antennae swiveling to and fro.

"My dad said he can paint"—Cheri consulted a notepad for the right word—*"concentric* rings on it. Like red in the middle for us and our dates, and a silver ring around the outer edge for, like, the losers? You and your hunk will dance in a gold circle in the very middle."

Libby nodded approvingly. "Fine. Photo areas?"

Cee Cee responded. "I've ordered three different backdrops: a castle court for us, a little peasant hut for nerds and geeks, and"—she couldn't resist laughing—"I ordered a medieval kitchen backdrop for the teachers and chaperons."

Everyone laughed except Sabrina. Even her proboscis didn't uncurl. She was getting angrier by the minute.

"Food?" Libby prompted.

A redheaded cheerleader held her hand up. "Under control. The caterer knows which table to put the good stuff on, and I've arranged for one of the servers to keep the freaks away from it."

"Perfect," Libby concluded. "All we need is to pick from our list of bands, which I'll do by tomorrow."

The girls applauded, and Libby smiled graciously.

"Now let's get to the public meeting. Remember what I said—no details. Don't give them anything to object to." Libby paused. "And watch out for Sabrina. She's been causing trouble lately."

As the cheerleaders trooped out of the bathroom, Sabrina-the-fly rubbed her hairy forelegs together in anticipation. "You ain't seen nothin' yet," she said in an itty-bitty fly voice.

* * *

Returning to human form, Sabrina found Valerie and Harvey at the door of the classroom where the meeting was to be held. Seeing Valerie was no surprise, but Sabrina hadn't expected Harvey.

He shuffled his feet, looking embarrassed. "Well, I thought that if the prom plans mattered so much to you, Sabrina, I should come, too—for moral support and all."

"Harvey, that's so sweet!" Sabrina wanted to kiss him, but figured it wouldn't be cool in front of Valerie, who still didn't have a prom date. So far Valerie hadn't mustered up the courage to ask Todd Earling—not that Todd was likely to get asked by any other girl. He wasn't a geek, but he wasn't a member of the social elite, either. He was one of those quiet, in-between guys that everybody vaguely remembered seeing but nobody really knew. Valerie had always thought he was cute, but she'd never done more than talk with him. Thinking about Valerie's datelessness made Sabrina all the more grateful that she'd found such a simpatico soul in Harvey. "Thanks," she said in response to his prom concerns. "I have a feeling we'll need all the support we can get."

"For what?" Valerie asked curiously.

"Uh . . . to help out . . . if they need help." Sabrina herded her friends forward. "C'mon, let's go inside."

Several students had already taken seats in the roped-off section of the room. As Sabrina sat down among them, Libby and her entourage entered and took their places at the front of the room. "I call this meeting of the Westbridge High Prom Planning Committee to order," said Libby. "First order of business: the prom theme."

One by one the cheerleaders gave their reports, but only Sabrina knew the objectionable details they were carefully omitting. By the time Jill stood up to talk about decorations, Sabrina's fists were clenched in her lap and her jaw hurt from gritting her teeth. Valerie chose that moment to lean over and whisper, "You know, I hate to admit it, but these guys sound really organized."

"You have no idea," Sabrina whispered back.

"Excuse me, Sabrina, did you just volunteer?"

The teenage witch looked up to find Libby gazing directly at her. "Huh?"

Libby milked the moment. "I just called for volunteers to help Jill with the decorations. Specifically, we need common laborers to build a big papier-mâché dragon. You'd be perfect to make the red crepe paper fire—the job requires someone intimately acquainted with dragon breath."

Sabrina felt like a volcano about to erupt. Valerie came to her rescue. "I'll help," she said. "I'm good with dragon breath." She paused. "Wait, should I admit that?"

Several other students raised their hands to volunteer as well, and Sabrina finally lost control. She jumped to her feet. "Can't you guys see what's happening? Libby's organizing everything to favor the cheerleaders and the football players, and the rest of us are going to get gypped! You think you're participating in your prom, but what you're really doing is supporting Libby Chessler's ego fest!"

The cheerleaders started to babble angrily, but Libby held up her hand. "I don't know what you're talking about, Sabrina," she said calmly.

"What I'm talking about, Libby, is that you've already chosen yourself to be prom queen, you've ordered special food just for you and your friends, and you're going to make the rest of us have our prom pictures taken in front of a peasant hut!"

At times like these, Libby was her own worst enemy. So stunned was she to hear all her secret plans revealed that her face actually paled. The students in the roped-off section began to mutter suspiciously.

Quickly Libby recovered her composure. With a superior smirk, she said, "If anyone wants to debate morals and ethics with Sabrina Spellman, please do so after the meeting. Right now we have more important things to do."

"What's more important than being fair?" Sabrina demanded. "I demand fair representation—like me and Valerie. If you don't let us join the committee, we'll . . . we'll . . . we'll organize our own prom!"

Chapter 5

☆

☆

That announcement took Valerie by surprise. "We will?" she gasped.

"Yes," said Sabrina. "We'll organize an anti-prom that'll take place at the exact same time as the spring prom." Caught up in the drama of the confrontation, she added, "So there!" before she realized how dorky it sounded.

Once again Libby paled. How could she lord it over the nerds, geeks, and freaks at the prom if they *weren't at* the prom? Libby knew her nemesis well enough to recognize a genuine threat. Determined to defuse the situation, she said, "That's stupid. There's no such thing as an anti-prom, so you can't hold one."

"Why not? There's no law that says students have to attend the official prom. If we don't like yours, we can organize our own. Right, Val?"

With a deer-caught-in-the-headlights expression, Valerie answered, "Uh . . . right."

"And I'll help them," Harvey chimed in.

Libby felt the threat increasing instead of being defused. "Harvey, you wouldn't dare go to a freak prom," she declared. "Nobody would."

"If we organize it, they will come," Sabrina retorted.

"You don't have enough time."

"We'll work fast."

Libby glared. Sabrina waited. For a fleeting moment, she felt as if she should be wearing a six-shooter at her hip and standing in the dusty main street of Dodge City.

But instead of going for a fast draw, Libby suddenly sat back in her chair. "Unlike you," she said, "I have had extensive experience in organizing popular social events. I know how much skill it requires, and I'd hate to see you fail miserably, which you inevitably would. So to save you from the humiliation, Sabrina, I've decided to let you join the committee."

All Sabrina said was "And Valerie, too."

Libby waved a hand. "Whatever."

The last thing Sabrina expected to hear was applause, but that's exactly what filled the room. Everybody in the roped-off section of the classroom stood up and cheered. Sabrina flushed with triumph as the story of David and Goliath flashed through her mind—only her version of Goliath wore a cheerleader's uniform.

Libby realized she had lost the moment, so with a scowl she stood up. "Meeting adjourned," she snapped. The committee filed out.

Sabrina headed for the door, followed by exclamations of "Way to go, Spellman!" and "Good move, Sabrina!" Valerie gave her a hug. Harvey smiled with admiration.

Sabrina had to admit that she felt a little lightheaded. Dealing with Libby was always a chore, but this situation was different. Whether or not the other students were aware of it, Sabrina was fighting for more than just the prom. This victory was a statement not simply of teenage fairness but of fairness and equality in general.

It was a good thing she didn't hear Libby's quiet remark to the other committee members: "We'll let them choose the napkins."

Sabrina hurried home, eager to tell her aunts all about her victory. Happily bounding up the front steps, she pulled the door open, burst through, and promptly fell into a hole. "Aaagh!"

The next thing she knew, she was sprawled in moist, freshly turned dirt. "Oh, yuck! There goes my blouse." She sat up and regarded the dirt walls of her hole—they were over six feet high. It wasn't quite as weird as the time she'd come home to find the house infested with giant Other Realm spiders, but it was weird enough. "Aunt Zelda!" she called out. "Aunt Hilda! There's a hole in the floor and I'm stuck in it!"

No answer.

"Yoo-hoo, anybody home up there?"

Silence. Sabrina looked around and realized she wasn't really in a hole; it was a long ditch. About seven feet deep, it started just inside the front door, ran down the hall, and continued straight into the kitchen, where it ended at the breakfast table. And at the far end she made a frightening discovery: Hilda, standing as stiff as a statue, her eyes glazed over, her expression a complete blank.

"Aunt Hilda, are you okay?"

"Mmf . . . mfpth . . ." Hilda tried to say, and then an extraordinary thing happened—an otherworldly bell clanged, green smoke billowed all over the place, and Hilda turned to wood. Smooth as a table now and about as thick as a copy of *War and Peace,* she quietly toppled over and fell flat on her wooden face.

Sabrina gasped. "Aunt Hilda!" With effort, she managed to get her unwieldy aunt upright again. "Omigosh, she's turned into a door or something! I've got to save her!" Trying not to panic, Sabrina struggled to think of an appropriate incantation.

Uhh—three, six, nine, ten,
Make Aunt Hilda normal again.

It didn't make much sense, but at least it rhymed. Sabrina pointed her finger at Hilda, expecting to feel that familiar rush of witch magic flow out from her fingertip, but nothing happened. No smoke, no sparkles, not even a wheezy cough. She shook her hand and tried again. No luck. "It's not me; it's this hole," she suddenly realized. "It's like a magical vacuum down here."

"I wouldn't be surprised if that's exactly what it is," came a familiar drawl. Salem's fuzzy black head appeared over the lip of the hole, his wide golden eyes peering down at her. "I'd say it was nice of you to drop in, but you probably wouldn't appreciate the irony."

"No, Salem, I wouldn't," Sabrina said. "Where have you been? Didn't you hear me call?"

"Yes and no," Salem answered carefully. "I was on the phone with the Other Realm Community Service Appointment Bureau, and I couldn't exactly put them on hold."

"Oh, but it was okay to let me stand here, trapped and screaming?"

"Well, the bureau is a busy place," said Salem. "On the other hand, I knew you weren't going anywhere."

"Thanks a lot. Now can you get me out of here?"

Salem pointed a paw at himself. *"Moi?* Who do you think I am, Rin-Tin-Cat? If I had the strength to get you out, I'd be able to open tuna cans—and you can imagine which trick I'd be doing right now."

Sabrina gestured at the oversize grave around her. "Then can you at least explain why a giant ditch is in the house and why Hilda's turned into a piece of wood?"

"Hilda made the rut," Salem explained. "Zelda went off on a shopping trip, and Hilda was so angry that she couldn't go along, she started to pace back and forth between the door and the kitchen."

Sabrina's eyes bugged. "She made this hole by *walking?*"

"It's not a hole. It's a rut, as in *stuck in*. Get it?"

Now it made sense, in a bizarre witchy way. "Aunt Hilda got stuck in a rut!"

"Exactly. But I have no idea how she turned to wood. Maybe she played too many *board* games." He chuckled at his joke.

Sabrina was too busy looking around the rut to laugh. "My magic can't work in a rut, the walls are too high to climb, and there's nothing in here for me to use to get out," she said. "Salem, can you bring me a rope?"

"What good will that do? I can't pull you up any more than I can tie the other end to a table leg." He held up a paw. "Just call me Stubby."

Sabrina thought hard. "Then bring me the phone."

"Sorry, I can't reach the cordless phone, and the other one's too heavy for me to lift. I've tried doing push-ups, but it just doesn't work when you've got detached shoulder blades."

"Then *you* use the phone. I know you can dial

it. Call the police. Call the fire department. Call somebody!"

"And say what?" Salem asked reasonably. " 'Hi, I'm a cat and I need you to rescue two witches out of a hole in a kitchen floor? And by the way, one of the witches is made of wood'?"

Sabrina had to admit he had a point. "Then how about this: bring me some paper and a pen, and I'll write a note asking for help. Then you can sort of conveniently drop it on the neighbors' doorstep and ring the bell."

"No can do," Salem said. "I've got to go to the Other Realm now to do my community service. If I'm late, it'll go on my record, and you know how pristine that is." He started to leave, then turned back. "See? Now you know why it's so hard to get out of a rut."

Sabrina couldn't believe that Salem would just leave her there. "Salem, come back! Don't you dare—"

A loud thump followed by a feminine cry of "Aaargh!" interrupted her.

"Oh, good," Sabrina said, "Aunt Zelda must be home."

Chapter 6

☆

☆

Sabrina hurried to the far end of the rut to find Zelda on her hands and knees in the dirt, surrounded by an assortment of shopping bags. "Goodness gracious, what happened?" Zelda exclaimed, staring at all the dirt. "I just walked in the door and almost broke my leg!"

The words tumbled out of Sabrina. "Aunt Hilda got stuck in a rut and our magic won't work in it and Salem won't help and Aunt Hilda's turned into a piece of lumber!"

Zelda's eyes actually crossed. "Wait a minute, slow down," she ordered, getting to her feet and dusting herself off. "Now try it again."

"I said, Aunt Hilda got stuck in a rut and our magic won't work in it and Salem won't help and Aunt Hilda's turned into a piece of lumber!"

"That's what I thought you said." She rushed

over to Hilda, who was as wooden as ever. "Oh, dear," Zelda said, "I was afraid this might happen."

Freaking out at this point, Sabrina asked, "What? What?"

"Being grounded is just too much for poor Hilda. She got bored."

Sabrina blinked. "Bored? That's it? She gets bored and so she turns *into* a board? Why does magic always involve stupid puns?"

"It's not about puns, Sabrina. It's just that we witches respond to stress in different ways," Zelda explained. "Hilda has a very low tolerance for restriction and a high tolerance for really bad puns."

Both statements were true, Sabrina knew. She'd often thought of Hilda as her "wild aunt," and as far as Hilda's tolerance for bad puns was concerned . . . well, Sabrina shuddered remembering the time Hilda suffered from an attack of pun-itis that made every pun she uttered become a physical reality. *At least she never complained of feeling as if she had the weight of the world on her shoulders,* Sabrina thought. *Who knows what might have happened?* "So what's going to happen to me if I get stressed?" she asked. "I'll crack down the middle?"

"Be careful," warned Zelda. "You might. You'll feel better once we get out of this rut, but first we've got to get Hilda out."

Together they managed to pick up the wooden witch and push her up over the lip of the rut. Then Zelda laced her fingers together and offered Sabrina a leg up.

Scrambling against the crumbling dirt, Sabrina finally made it out, but she ruined her jeans doing it. Zelda's clothes didn't suffer as much, since Sabrina was able to pull her up quite easily. "Now how do we get rid of the rut?" Sabrina asked.

Barely did she get the question out when the floor from door to kitchen magically repaired itself.

"See? You don't have to," Zelda said. "Once you get out of a rut, it ceases to exist. But our initial problem isn't solved. Now we need to throw a party, and fast."

Sabrina wasn't sure if she'd heard what she thought she'd just heard. "Did you say we have to throw a . . . party? Now?"

Zelda propped Hilda up against the counter. "The only way to snap Hilda back to normal is to catch her interest and keep her from becoming bored again. One of the most interesting things to Hilda is a party, so we're going to have a party."

Sabrina shrugged. "For almost two weeks? Cool!"

Zelda shook her head. "I don't know about the full time she's grounded, but we'll have to maintain it for at least a few hours. Now, let me see . . ." With a flick of her finger, she magically decorated the kitchen like an island paradise, with real jungle plants growing right up out of the floor, a bubbling waterfall outside the glass-paneled door, a coconut centerpiece on the counter, colorful streamers, lights and—

"Monkeys!" Sabrina cried out as a group of furry little animals leaped like manic gymnasts from one tree to another. One landed on her head and pulled playfully at her hair, chitting and yipping. "Hey, get off me!"

The monkey leaped away just as an enormous macaw flew by in a streak of neon colors. It landed on top of the straw hut that now housed the refrigerator and squawked so loud that Sabrina put her hands over her ears.

Zelda continued to point her finger: a reggae band appeared and began to play; a crowd of happy guests materialized and milled around; and Sabrina suddenly found herself wearing a grass skirt and a bikini top. "That's the spirit," Zelda said, zapping herself into a similar outfit. "Have fun! The more fun we have, the more Hilda will want to join us!" She swayed to the music.

Sabrina was already tapping her foot to the beat. "If I have to party hard in the hope of saving Aunt Hilda, who am I to argue?" With a whoop she and Zelda started a conga line that snaked its way out of the kitchen, up the stairs, through all the bedrooms and back down again. When they reentered the kitchen, Hilda was waiting for them, decked out in a grass skirt and grinning, all signs of "board-dom" gone.

"What a great party!" Hilda exclaimed. "Can I lead the conga line, please-please-please?"

"Be my guest!" Sabrina gladly gave up the post when the phone started to ring. At least, she thought it was the phone. The music was so loud it might have been her head ringing. "I'll get the phone, Aunt Zelda!" she shouted over the band. "It's good to have you back, Aunt Hilda!"

"It's good to be back!" whooped Hilda, and merrily led the conga line out of the kitchen again.

Sabrina picked up the phone. "Hello?"

Somebody said something, but there was too much noise for Sabrina to be sure what. She hurried into the dining room and closed the door, but not before the macaw flew in after her. "Hello?" she said again into the phone.

"Sabrina?" It was Harvey. "What's all the racket? Sounds like you're having a wild party over there."

"No, it's just"—Sabrina thought frantically—"my aunt Hilda's birthday. It's not really a big deal. She's just gets . . . excited." The macaw chose that moment to squawk so loud that Harvey must have heard it. "That wasn't a real bird," Sabrina told him quickly. "It's a sound-effects CD—one of my aunt's presents."

Harvey grunted. "You must have a good sound system. That was so loud it hurt my ears."

"Sorry. So," Sabrina prompted him, "what's up?"

"Oh, that's right—I called you." Harvey's voice became glum. "I just wanted to give you the bad news."

"Uh-oh. What bad news?"

Harvey sighed. "My dad just got a brilliant idea. At least, he thinks it's brilliant. He sort of maneuvered me into wearing his old prom tux to our spring prom. He's had it packed away for years in a bag filled with nitrogen."

"Nitrogen?"

"Yeah, from his extermination company. It not only kills bugs; it also preserves clothes. So now he wants to air his tux out and pass it on to me."

Sabrina tried to be positive. "What's wrong with that? It's kind of cute, in a generation-gap sort of way."

"You're forgetting when my dad went to his high school prom, Sabrina—in the early 1970s."

Sabrina's mind whirled. The 1970s. The age of disco and "Have a nice day" and puka shell necklaces and— "It's not made out of polyester, is it?"

"Yeah," Harvey confessed glumly, "it is. Powder blue. And it has a big yellow smiley face stitched on the pocket."

"I'm gonna faint." Even Zelda's festive party decorations and the enthusiastic reggae band in the kitchen didn't stop Sabrina's knees from wobbling. "You can't wear a power-blue polyester tux to the spring prom! You'll look like a bad Ken doll!"

It was hard to tell over the phone which emotion Harvey was feeling most strongly—guilt or revulsion. "I've got no choice, Sabrina," he said in a strained voice. "Believe me, I tried to talk him out of it, but you know my dad: he gets these weird ideas and nothing and no one can change his mind."

"But it's not fair!" Sabrina wailed.

"You know that and I know that," Harvey said. *"He* doesn't know that."

Sabrina wanted to go on talking to Harvey, but the macaw started squawking again and the reggae band cranked up their volume, adding to her own growing gloom. She finally told Harvey she had to hang up. Her mood wasn't helped when she went back to the kitchen to find a note in the toaster—or rather, in the coconut-shaped object that served as a toaster for the duration of Hilda's party. Sabrina snatched the note up and went back to the dining room to read it.

The note read itself to her, in Vesta's familiar voice: "Sabrina, dear, I'll be popping in tomorrow evening to discuss your prom wardrobe. See you then!"

Sabrina flopped down into a chair. "Great. Harvey's dad is making him wear a moldy old tux, and Aunt Vesta will probably try to make me wear black leather. What a pair we're going to make."

Somehow Sabrina didn't feel like partying anymore.

☆

Chapter 7

☆

Hilda's party continued long into the night, but Sabrina locked herself in her room after Harvey's phone call. Zelda was worn out after a few hours and went to bed, leaving Hilda alone with her magical guests—after Zelda zapped a soundproof barrier around the first floor.

The next morning Sabrina dragged herself out of bed, her thoughts haunted by a series of horrible dreams she'd had about prom night, most of them involving Harvey in a stretch polyester tux and Sabrina in an outfit better suited for Catwoman. In one dream she almost died of asphyxiation because the leather was too tight. In another dream she got thrown out of the prom for indecent exposure and Harvey became a laughing-stock. In yet another dream they were crowned king and queen of the freaks and were strapped to a wall so that Libby's crowd could throw water balloons at them.

Needless to say, Sabrina hadn't slept well.

"What am I going to do, Salem?" she asked the cat while putting the finishing touches on her makeup for school. "No matter what kind of dress I wear, Harvey's going to look like a dork, which means both of us will look like dorks." The thought of Libby laughing at her and throwing water balloons at her was too much to bear.

"That's one good thing—maybe the only good thing—about being a cat," Salem replied. "I don't have to get dressed, and I always complement the decor."

"Yeah, but you get fleas."

"Well, there you go. No outfit is perfect."

Sabrina didn't get much more sympathy downstairs. Hilda had a horrible headache from partying too hard, which irritated Zelda, who was left to clean up the house. "I knew there was a reason why we didn't throw parties anymore," she grumbled, walking from room to room with a big plastic trash bag she zapped up to collect the garbage. Her eyes lit up when she spotted Sabrina. "Sabrina, would you be a dear and zap all those dishes into the sink? I'll point them clean later."

"Why doesn't Aunt Hilda do it?" Sabrina whined. "It was her party, and I have to go to school."

Hilda was draped on the couch like a dying

soprano in a grand opera, except that her moaning wasn't musical and she held a big ice pack to her head. "It's not faaaiiirr. . . ."

"I'll say," Sabrina snapped, grudgingly zapping up plates and cups from every corner of the living room. "When I went to bed, the house was still relatively clean."

"No, I mean, why does a really good evening have to mean a bad headache the next morning?" moaned Hilda. "Why do fun things always create un-fun consequences? You fry food nice and crispy, you get fat. You eat chocolate, you break out. You find a date, he stands you up."

"You get bored, you turn into wood," Sabrina added, gingerly zapping away a used napkin.

"Sorry about that, by the way," Hilda said. "I was never good at being grounded." Her wince of pain softened into a smile. "Thanks for the party, Sabrina. You and Zelda saved me from a future of endless board-dom."

Hilda's apology melted some of Sabrina's irritation. "That's okay. You didn't mean to turn to wood. I'm just annoyed by a lot of stuff right now." She threw the napkin away, finished collecting dirty dishes, and zapped them into the sink. "I'm done, Aunt Zelda," she called upstairs. "I've got to go now or I'll miss the bus."

"Have a good day at school," Zelda said. "And whatever you do, don't let the monkeys out. I haven't zapped them back to the jungle yet."

As if they'd heard her, several little monkeys

scampered out of the hall closet and ran to the door, as if waiting for Sabrina to open it. "Nice try, guys," she told them, and then she pointed her finger and froze them for a count of ten. During that count, she slipped outside.

When Sabrina got to school, she discovered that things weren't much better there. True, she and Valerie were scheduled to attend their first Prom Planning Committee meeting, but already Sabrina was seeing bad signs about that.

"Good morning, freakettes," Libby greeted them in the hall. "By the way, the meeting time has been changed from after school to during lunch. I hope you happened to bring a sack lunch today, because you won't have time to go to the cafeteria." She waved her own lunch bag, as did her friends, and they all walked away, laughing.

Sabrina couldn't zap up something for them to eat or Val would be suspicious.

"Maybe Mrs. Poopypants will let us get something to go," Sabrina said hopefully, not knowing that the lunch lady was walking by at that moment.

"I keep telling you, my name is *Poopiepentz!*" the woman growled.

Valerie sighed. "There goes any chance of a meal-to-go."

At lunchtime Sabrina and Valerie, both with growling stomachs, joined the Prom Planning Committee in Mrs. Quick's math classroom. The cheerleaders were already there, daintily eating from an assortment of packed foods. "Look who's decided to show up," said Cee Cee, making a show of biting into a fried chicken leg.

"You're late," Jill said, munching salad out of a plastic bowl. "This committee does not tolerate tardiness."

Sabrina held back any comment while Valerie cringed in silence. Obviously the cheerleaders had somehow gotten out of their previous classes early, just so they could pull this stunt, but Sabrina wasn't about to rise to their bait. Maybe she couldn't zap in an instant lunch without attracting attention, but she could still pretend. "Sorry we're late. Val and I just finished eating lunch." Turning to Valerie, she added, "Boy, that lasagna was good, wasn't it?"

Thank goodness Valerie caught on. "Lasagna?" she asked, looking hungry. Then she blurted, "Oh! Yes, the lasagna." She feigned a little burp. "It was the best."

Libby scrutinized the two of them, but Sabrina only smiled. "Okay," Sabrina said, "so what's first on the agenda?"

"Actually," said Libby, putting down a half-eaten turkey sandwich, "most of the details are already taken care of. We've recruited enough manual labor for the dragon decoration, and the rest of the decorations will be handled by Jill's team. As far as the band goes, I've decided to hire Mayday Heyday for the dance, and the music department's Renaissance ensemble will play for the coronation ceremony and the king and queen's solo dance."

Valerie was trying not to drool at the sight of Libby's sandwich. "Wait a minute," she managed to say. "You're going to use Renaissance music at a prom with a Camelot theme?"

Libby's eyes narrowed. "Are nerds hard of hearing, too?"

"But, Libby, King Arthur didn't live during the Renaissance. He was born eight or nine hundred years earlier."

Libby just stared at her.

Valerie pressed on. "The music of his time was totally different."

Libby stared.

Valerie started to wither. "I mean, it would be historically inaccurate, which would be . . . you know . . . historically inaccurate. . . ."

Libby stared.

Valerie cringed and stepped back so that she could hide behind Sabrina. "Never mind, it was a stupid objection."

Libby stared.

Cee Cee tapped her shoulder. "You won, Libby."

"What?" Libby gave a little shake, as if coming out of a daydream. "Oh, good. Now, since the music is taken care of, the only other detail left to decide is the napkins." She smiled sweetly at Sabrina. "You two can handle that. Your choice of colors will be white and . . . white."

That did it. Sabrina's patience snapped. "And what about the duel?" she demanded.

Libby gave a little start. "Wh-what did you say?"

"I heard something about a duel between two knights for the honor of being crowned king of the prom," Sabrina said casually. "I would think it's pretty important to you, since you're already the queen."

Valerie's jaw dropped. "Sabrina, what are you talking about?"

"Just something a little fly told me," Sabrina replied, enjoying Libby's shock.

"Special entertainment issues are not your concern," Libby snapped. "And whatever you've heard, just forget it. Is that clear?"

Amused, Sabrina held up her hands. "I've wiped it from my mind."

"Wait," Valerie said, totally lost. "What's going on?"

"Nothing." Libby snatched up her half sandwich and dropped it into her lunch bag. "This meeting is adjourned. Thanks for coming. Goodbye."

The cheerleaders filed out.

Sabrina had won a battle, but she was far from winning the war. She sat on the grass in the school quad with Valerie and Harvey and complained, "This is so not fair! Why do I bother to care about being fair to people? Nobody else does—not

Libby, not Mr. Kraft, not your dad"—she gestured at Harvey—"and certainly not my aunts' dad." She thought of how Salem had abandoned her in the rut and thought, *Even the cat has no sense of justice.*

"Oh, come on, Sabrina, it's not that bad," said Harvey, ever the voice of reason during a tantrum. "We'll figure something out."

Sabrina slumped. "We'll figure something out" was often Harvey's way of saying, *"You'll* figure something out."

"Don't take it so hard," Valerie was saying. "Rejection isn't so bad. You can even get used to it. And personally, I think you did an excellent job getting this far with Libby."

"That's right," Harvey chimed in.

"But that's just it," Sabrina said. "I don't want to settle for *this far.* Nobody should have to *settle* for anything. Planning the prom should be a democratic operation. This is America, after all!"

"Yes, it certainly is," came an oily voice. "Land of the free and home of the brave, with equal opportunities for those of every *social stratum.*" Mr. Kraft walked up behind Sabrina and stood towering over her. "Do I have the pleasure of addressing the Superfluous Details Subcommittee?"

Sabrina almost choked. "The *what?*"

"I was given to understand that was your designation," said Kraft.

Sabrina, Valerie, and Harvey exchanged glances. "Libby," they concluded in unison.

"Yes, she told me I'd find you out here." Kraft held out a piece of paper. "Since you want to help with the prom so much, I thought you might enjoy a special task. This is a master copy of a letter that needs to be sent out to the parents of every student in the school. I've decided to recruit chaperons from among the parent population as well as the faculty."

Sabrina blanched, not knowing which fact horrified her most—the fact that she'd just inherited a rotten job, no doubt thanks to Libby, or the fact that the prom was going to be overflowing with parents.

When Sabrina didn't move, Kraft shook the letter. "Take it! This has to be in the mail today. You can use the copy machine in the office, and you'll find envelopes and stamps there as well. If you start immediately after your last class, you should be able to get them all out by the last mail pickup at the post office." He flashed a nasty little grin. "Granted, it would be cheaper to ask students to take the letters home with them, but I'm no fool—no teenager with half a brain would ask their parents to chaperon the prom."

Dumbstruck, Sabrina took the letter. Kraft sauntered away.

"I don't believe this," said Valerie. "This is so not fair!"

"You said it," Harvey moped.

Sabrina just fumed.

That night Sabrina sat on her bed, exhausted from copying, folding, addressing, and mailing hundreds of letters after having endured a full day at school. *There must be something I can do about all this,* she thought angrily. *There must be some way to make circumstances more fair.*

She opened up her magic book and consulted the index. She couldn't do anything about Hilda's predicament—that was Hilda's own fault—and the idea of magically messing with Harvey's dad made her a little nervous. But Libby Chessler? "It's open season on cheerleaders," Sabrina decided with a grin.

She found just the right potion and got to work preparing it.

☆

Chapter 8

☆

"Did you study for the English quiz?" Valerie asked the next morning, nervously clutching her schoolbooks as if that might make the information ooze out of the pages, seep through her skin, and flow directly into her brain.

Sabrina was standing by her locker and, startled by Valerie's voice, almost dropped the little glass jar in her hands. *No, don't break it!* she thought frantically, and fumbled it into her locker before Valerie could really see it. "I studied for a while," she blurted, "but all that mailing wiped me out. I went to bed kinda early." *After whipping up this potion,* she added to herself.

Valerie tried to peek inside Sabrina's locker. "What's that? A jar of mustard?"

Trying to be nonchalant about it, Sabrina

blocked Valerie's view. "Uh, yeah, that's just what it is—mustard. Dijon-style, actually. The cafeteria mustard is so dull, don't you think?"

"I never noticed." Valerie waved as Harvey approached. "Hi, Harvey. Did you study for the English quiz?"

"A little," Harvey replied, watching as Sabrina tried to sneak the glass jar into her jacket pocket. "What's that, Sabrina? Looks like mustard."

"It's Dijon-style mustard," Valerie explained, then gave Sabrina a quizzical look. "Why are you carrying it around?"

"Uh . . . I don't want to forget it for lunch." Sabrina closed her locker. "Look, I'll catch you guys in English, okay?"

"Okay," said Valerie. "We can all flunk the quiz together."

Sabrina hurried off, weaving her way down the crowded hall, her eyes searching for Libby and her cronies. She finally spotted them and quickly scuttled around a corner that gave her a good view of Libby while at the same time sheltering her from the gaze of passersby. She took the glass jar out of her pocket. Inside, a yellowish fog roiled around like a gaseous version of a lava lamp. *At a glance it does sort of look like mustard,* Sabrina thought, then poised her hand to open the lid. Recalling the instructions she'd read in her magic book the night before, she chanted a modified version of the activation spell:

66

In the name of the nerd, the freak, and the square,
I summon a wind that is truly fair.

She opened the jar.

With a gentle *whoosh,* the yellow air blew out, dissipating to the point where it was no longer visible. *The Fair Wind is blowing!* Sabrina thought. *Now let's see what it does to Libby.*

The Fair Wind blew past the cheerleaders, lightly ruffling their perfectly coiffed hair. Cee Cee glanced around. "What's with the air vents?"

"Never mind the air vents," Libby snapped, "just listen to me," and she went on talking.

I guess it needs time to work, Sabrina thought, remembering what her magic book had said: that the Boreas and Sons Fair Wind potion guaranteed results, though superior-minded, egotistical, and selfish people usually took longer than others to respond. *And Libby sure is superior-minded, egotistical, and selfish,* Sabrina thought.

She wondered how her nemesis would finally react. Libby would probably start by giving Sabrina a friendly greeting at their next committee meeting. Then she would demand a series of last-minute changes: no stupid duel, the same food for everyone, no sectioned-off dance areas, no status-oriented photo booths, and a fair election for the prom king and queen. "What a wonderful world it will be," Sabrina murmured happily to herself.

English class came and went, and to Sabrina's relief, the quiz wasn't the complete disaster that Valerie had predicted. In fact, afterward Valerie admitted, "I think I did okay, especially when Mrs. Reilly gave us that bonus question at the last minute."

"It's not like her to be so nice," noted Harvey, "but, boy, it'll save my grade. The points from the bonus question will make up for all the questions I got wrong."

Sabrina was about to comment when she felt something warm drift past, like a spring breeze. Mr. Kraft, who was just walking into his office, reached up to tidy his hair as it was gently ruffled out of place. Then he froze midway through the motion, as if an amazing idea had just occurred to him. Snapping back to life, he turned on his heel and headed straight for Sabrina and Valerie. "Miss Spellman and Miss Birkhead," he said, "am I ever glad I found you two. I just wanted to say thank you for sending out all those letters so efficiently. I think you're doing a splendid job on the Prom Planning Committee." And with that he returned to his office, stepped inside, and closed the door.

Valerie scratched her head. "What was that all about?"

"I'm not sure," said Sabrina, but she didn't have time to wonder about it as Todd Earling cautiously approached them.

"Uh, Valerie?" he said, sidling up to her. "I was

kind of wondering if you wanted to go to the spring prom with me. I mean, it's not too late to ask you, is it?"

Valerie nearly choked. "Late? No! Of course not! Yes! I'll go!" She swallowed, frantically trying to calm down. "I mean, sure, I'd love to go with you."

Todd nodded. "Great. 'Cause I've been wanting to ask you, but the thought of trying to look good at a prom with all the cool people kind of made me nervous. But now I think it's only fair that we nerds make our presence known. Right?"

"Err . . ." Valerie shrugged. "Sure. I guess."

"Great." Todd took a step back. "So I'll see you then?"

"Uh-huh," Valerie stammered. "I mean, yeah. I mean, *yes.*"

As Todd slunk away and Valerie stood frozen in utter shock, Sabrina's mind raced. Mrs. Reilly's uncharacteristically nice bonus question, Mr. Kraft's unexpected compliment, Todd Earling's sudden interest in Valerie—there could be only one explanation. *But I aimed the Fair Wind at Libby,* Sabrina thought. *Can it affect other people at the same time?*

The answer came immediately. The warm breeze blew past her again, then lifted up the skirt of a girl down the hall. The girl gave a startled "Eeep!" and pushed her skirt back down. Desmond Jacobi, jock extraordinaire, snickered.

Wait a minute—that's not fair at all! Sabrina

thought in irritation, until she saw Jacobi's startled expression as the Fair Wind gathered up his loose-fitting T-shirt and blew it up around his neck. A pack of freshman girls happened to be walking by, and they giggled. Desmond grabbed at his billowing shirt and pulled it back down. Sabrina grinned. *Okay,* that's *fair!*

Harvey was laughing. "I've never seen Jacobi blush before. Look at him—his cheeks are bright red."

Valerie had missed the whole thing. She was still in shock about Todd Earling. "He asked me out," she kept repeating. "This is so cool!"

Sabrina spotted Libby walking down the hall. "Excuse me a minute, guys," she told her friends, and hurried to catch up with the cheerleader. "Libby, can I talk to you a minute about the prom?"

Libby didn't stop walking. She didn't even turn around. "No" was all she said.

Sabrina sighed. *Well, that answers that. I guess the Fair Wind still needs more time.*

So she waited. Later, at lunch, she met Harvey at their usual table. "Have you noticed anything unusual about Libby?" she casually asked him.

"No," Harvey answered. "Why?"

"Oh . . . nothing."

Valerie angrily dropped her tray flat on the table and sat down. "It's mystery food again," she grumped. "Jeez, I hate this lumpy stuff!"

"It's the white sauce special," Harvey explained, and shoveled a forkful into his mouth. "Tastes okay to me."

"It looks like a chemistry class accident," said Sabrina, not anxious to eat the goop on her plate. Wednesday in the school cafeteria was known as Mystery Day—something in white sauce, but nobody could figure out what it was. Probably the leftovers from the day before, but why did Mrs. Poopiepentz have to make it look so disgusting?

"Just put ketchup on it" was Harvey's usual advice. "That way you'll at least get a vegetable serving."

Harvey, however, seemed to be the only person who could ingest that much ketchup and live. In minutes the cafeteria was filled with disgruntled students complaining about the food. "This is gross!" and "They can't force me to eat this!" and "Ewww!" finally brought out Mrs. Poopiepentz herself.

"Can I have everybody's attention, please?" she bellowed. "I understand there's some unrest about today's menu. I am sensitive to your needs and concerns, so please allow me to assure you that the creamy substance on your plates has indeed been approved by the State Board of Health—so *eat it!*"

The grumbling grew louder, and Sabrina feared the crowd would revolt when she felt a suspiciously warm breeze blow past. Mrs. Poopiepentz blinked rapidly a few times, then addressed the students again. "On the other hand, it's not really fair to make you eat pig slop every day, is it?"

The students, surprised by this sudden change in sentiment, cautiously muttered their agreement.

"I mean," Mrs. Poopiepentz went on thoughtfully, "you get no say whatsoever in the selection of foods or beverages in this institution."

A few more mutters of agreement.

Mrs. Poopiepentz came to a decision. "I hereby announce the beginning of a new system. Each week I'll take lunch orders and prepare meals as you specify."

Mr. Kraft just happened to walk in at that moment, and Sabrina thought his eyes were about to pop out. *"What?"* he shrilled, and pulled the lunch lady aside. "Are you crazy?" he demanded, shaking her.

The warm breeze blew past again.

Kraft blinked. "No, of course you're not crazy," he answered himself. "In fact, I think that's a wonderful idea!" He clapped his hands sharply to get everybody's attention. "Okay, kids, here's what we'll do: your homeroom teachers will take lunch orders every morning, and those orders will be passed on to Mrs. Poopiepentz. And to make sure that all the food is prepared on time and to your specifications, I'll hire a catering service to help. What do you think?"

The students roared their approval.

"I don't believe this," said Libby, standing up to face Kraft. "I've been asking for a catering service for the cheerleaders for months, but you never listened to me."

Kraft beamed at her. "Well, now you have it. Enjoy!" He and Mrs. Poopiepentz left.

"But it's not fair!" Libby said, running after them. "It was my idea! If anybody is to get catered food, it should be the cheerleaders!"

The crowd booed her as she left. Then everybody rejoiced at the new lunch plan. Only Sabrina sat in silence, totally confused. A catered lunch service was cool beyond words, yes, but Libby still wasn't being affected by the Fair Wind. *Why?*

By the end of the day, Sabrina had witnessed the Fair Wind stop a fight between two students, make a senior share his candy bar with a freshman, and cause Jill and Cee Cee to say a cheerful hi to Valerie. But Libby still remained good old I'm-better-than-thou Libby. "I don't get it," Sabrina muttered.

"What?" asked Valerie.

They stood in front of the mirror in the girls' bathroom, combing their hair. Classes were over, and it was almost time for the Prom Planning Committee meeting. Sabrina had suggested they spruce up beforehand, not only to look up-to-par on the cheerleader primp scale but also to keep Libby from holding another secret meeting in the bathroom.

Sabrina gazed at her worried expression in the mirror. Would Libby ever respond to the Fair Wind? If not, there was no hope for the prom. Sabrina suddenly knew what she had to do. "Val, you go on ahead without me. I'll be with you in a second."

"Okay," Valerie said, and left.

Once Sabrina was alone, she took the glass jar from her pocket and opened it. Concentrating, she summoned the Fair Wind back to her. Within seconds a warm breeze blew in under the door, gathered itself into a yellowish haze, and zipped back into the jar. Sabrina screwed the lid on. "Maybe I should open the jar in Libby's face," she mused aloud, then shook her head. "No, too obvious. How about I duplicate it? Two Fair Winds are stronger than one." But she remembered that the potion required several hours to ferment before the Fair Wind could be released. She didn't have time to create a second one.

Then a sneaky smile crept over her face. "I know. I'll use a doubling spell! That way I don't have to create anything new." Sabrina pointed her finger at the jar and chanted:

A second Fair Wind is too much trouble; it
Works just to take the first one and double it!

The jar in her hands trembled, its mustard-yellow contents growing darker, roiling around inside like an angry storm. Without warning, the lid of the jar popped off and the super Fair Wind blew around the bathroom. "Whoa, that's some doubling spell!" Sabrina yelped, watching as the yellow haze dissipated and slid out under the door. "Go get her, tiger!" she called after it. Anticipating some fun ahead, she headed for the meeting room.

There she found Libby and the cheerleaders waiting. Valerie was there, too, trying not to look like she was there. *Only Valerie can feel alone in a roomful of people,* Sabrina thought, then said aloud, "Sorry I'm late, everybody. I was putting on lip gloss."

"It didn't help," Libby said flatly. "Now can we get on with it, please? We cheerleaders have practice afterward."

Sabrina couldn't resist such an easy comeback. "It won't help."

Libby glowered, but let the gibe slide by. "I call this meeting of the Prom Planning Committee to order. First, an announcement: since the prom is only three days away, tomorrow's meeting will be the last planning meeting. Everything's under control, thanks to my brilliant leadership."

Valerie timidly raised her hand. "Then why are we meeting?"

"Because I said so," Libby replied. "And because I . . ." She paused as a warm wind blew past. "That is, I . . ."

"You wanted to tell us all about that duel you had planned," Sabrina prompted, barely holding back a grin.

Libby's eyes clouded over with a yellowish haze, then cleared. She smiled. "You know, I was thinking it might be better to hold an election for the king and queen during the prom itself. Students could nominate their favorites, and the voting could be done by applause. Whoever gets the most applause wins then and there. That's fair, isn't it?"

Cee Cee nodded thoughtfully. "Definitely," she agreed.

"Besides," said Jill, "I was having trouble finding swords that Mr. Kraft would approve for the duel."

"Excellent!" said Libby. "Oh, and by the way, I want the food on all the tables mixed so that everyone has the same selections. That way we'll all get a little of everything."

"Check," Jill acknowledged, and scribbled on her notepad.

"What about, you know, the dance floor?" Cheri asked. "Should we, like, keep the dance zones and everything?"

"Of course," answered Libby.

Sabrina tensed. *Keep the dance zones? She shouldn't want to do that; it's unfair!*

"It still makes a great floor decoration, and

maybe we can hold a dance contest. The winners could be spotlight dancers in the middle."

"Cool!" the cheerleaders chimed.

By now Valerie's jaw had practically dropped to the floor. "Okay, this is a joke, right? You guys are just teasing us, right?"

With an earnest expression, Libby placed her hand on Valerie's shoulder. "Don't be so paranoid, Valerie. We're your friends, and everything's under control. We're going to have the best prom ever. And since Todd asked you out, you'll even be there!"

Valerie couldn't help but grin at that. "Yeah, I will, won't I?" she said dreamily, then snapped back to reality. "But I still don't understand why you're being so . . . nice."

Libby's smile was radiant. "Because it's only fair." She motioned the cheerleaders to her side and said, "Now we need to practice our cheers for tomorrow's game. Sabrina, Valerie, I look forward to seeing you in the morning."

"Good-bye!" the cheerleaders chorused, and left.

Looking as if she might faint, Valerie swayed in her chair. Sabrina steadied her. "See, Val? We joined the committee and look what's happened—Libby Chessler has seen the light!"

Chapter 9

☆

The Fair Wind had done its job, so Sabrina stayed behind after the committee meeting to gather it back up into its jar. But when she tried to summon it, nothing happened. By four-thirty she had looked everywhere on the school grounds without success.

She didn't worry about it. Her magic book had said that a Fair Wind usually lasted about twenty-four hours. By the time she returned to school the next morning, it would be gone. With her jar empty and her spirits high, she headed home.

She walked in the door to find Hilda and Zelda reading a letter—and not just any letter. "Mr. Kraft's letter!" she gasped when she saw it.

Hilda nodded. "What a neat idea, asking us to chaperon the prom." She nudged Zelda in the ribs. "Won't that be fun?"

Zelda was busy examining the envelope. "How odd. No postmark."

Uh-oh!

Sabrina blanched. Then in quick succession the expression on her face shifted from shock to guilt to panic, and she ended the series by trying very hard to appear casually uninterested.

It didn't work. Hilda noticed. "Sabrina, is something wrong?"

Sabrina gulped. "Wrong? No! Nothing's wrong. Everything's great. I'm going up to my room to study now." And she ran upstairs.

Closing the door of her bedroom, she faced the black cat lying on her bed. "How could this have happened, Salem? Aunt Hilda and Aunt Zelda just got a letter that I purposely *didn't* send to them!"

Salem, who had been napping, raised his head and yawned. "I once got punished for stealing catnip that I never got to eat."

"Salem, I'm serious!"

"So am I."

"Oh, never mind." Sabrina began to pace. "I can't panic. The whole thing with Libby is under control, so now I just have to deal with my aunts as chaperons and Harvey wearing a dorky tux"— her eyes bugged wide—"and Aunt Vesta! Oh, no, I forgot all about Aunt Vesta! She's coming over tonight to help me pick out a dress!"

"What's so bad about that?" asked Salem. "If there's one thing Vesta's got, it's fashion sense."

"Maybe, but she doesn't have any other kind of sense," Sabrina added, wringing her hands as she paced. "I've got to do something, but what?"

Salem gave her one of those kitty grins that tended to scare the neighbors. "Why don't you use some of that Fair Wind potion you made?"

Sabrina eyed him. "How do you know about that? I closed the door so nobody would see."

Nonchalant as ever, Salem licked a paw. "Never underestimate the snooping abilities of a cat."

Sabrina considered Salem's suggestion. Normally she didn't put spells on either Hilda or Zelda. They were her guardians and it just wouldn't have been right. But Aunt Vesta the uninvited busybody? "You'll have to sneak me some of the ingredients, Salem. If Aunt Hilda and Aunt Zelda see me get all of them, they'll know I'm up to something."

"Whereas they know I'm always up to something," Salem said. "All right, what do you need?"

Sabrina opened her magic book, and they got to work.

A short time later the potion was finished and Sabrina was called downstairs to dinner. She ate, cleaned up the kitchen, tried to act casual with her aunts for a bit, and then raced back upstairs to check the potion. "Rats. It's not ready, and Aunt Vesta will be here any minute." She cringed as a loud thunderclap sounded from the linen closet. "Double rats, she's here *now!*"

Like Cleopatra presenting herself to the crowds,

Vesta threw open the linen closet door and stepped out. Dressed in a skintight black leather pant suit, black boots, and a bouffant hairdo, she looked like a combination of a 1950s biker babe and a 1990s thrill-seeker. She held her arms out to her niece. "Sabrina! Darling!"

Sabrina dutifully gave her a hug and one of those annoying air kisses. "Hi, Aunt Vesta."

Vesta pointed her finger, and a huge stack of magazines floated out of the closet. "I thought we'd check out the major dress catalogs before making any decisions," she said. "I just love catalogs. If it's in fashion, it's in a catalog. Come along."

Vesta started downstairs, but Sabrina hung back. Snatching the little jar from her pocket, she opened it and quickly chanted,

Fair Wind, get me out of this mess.
Don't let Aunt Vesta choose my dress.

The pale yellow contents of the jar whispered out and followed Vesta, though Sabrina wondered if the potion was strong enough yet to have any effect. *I'll just have to keep my fingers crossed,* she thought, adding aloud to Salem in her bedroom, "Keep your paws crossed."

"Just don't ask me to keep my eyes crossed or I'll fall off the bed," the cat responded.

As Sabrina reached the kitchen she heard Hilda's voice. "Oh, gee, it's our eldest sister." Hilda emphasized the word *eldest* and added, "And look—she's wearing leather again."

"Hello, Hilda dear," Vesta said, giving Hilda a tight smile that indicated she'd heard the word "eldest" quite clearly. "Zelda darling, how are you?"

Zelda waved her hands, which were encased in kitchen mitts. "Hi, Vesta. Please excuse my lack of hands. I'm about to take some cookies out of the oven. Want one?"

"Heavens no, I only allow myself to eat sugar once a week." Vesta patted her perfectly flat tummy. "Must keep the figure in shape."

"If you want to wear that sausage suit, you do," Hilda muttered.

Sabrina cleared her throat. "Excuse me, but I think I ought to make it clear that I'm not sure what kind of prom dress I'll be wearing and I'm not really ready to make the decision tonight."

"Well, for heaven's sake, how long are you going to wait?" asked Vesta. "This is Wednesday already. Isn't the prom this Saturday?"

"Yes," admitted Sabrina, "but with magic to help, I still have plenty of time to decide."

Vesta headed for the living room, her stack of catalogs floating behind her. "Never leave to chance what can make or break your social standing," she advised.

"In other words, go pick out a dress," Hilda translated.

A hot cookie sheet in her hands, Zelda said

sympathetically, "There's no way out of it, Sabrina. When it comes to fashion, Vesta will not take no for an answer."

"This is the woman who, as a child, tried to market a line of Other Realm clothes using me as her display mannequin," said Hilda. "To this day my neck still hurts from holding those poses for so long."

"You might as well take advantage of her expertise, because she won't leave until you do," Zelda finished.

Realizing that her newest Fair Wind potion wasn't going to do her any good, Sabrina dutifully trudged into the living room.

Vesta already had all of the catalogs open, floating in the air around the room. The pages flipped slowly as she walked from one to the other, studying pictures. "Let's start with the major considerations," she said. "What kind of tux is your date, that Harvey mortal fellow, wearing?"

"That's a good question," said Sabrina, floundering for some way to avoid mentioning Harvey's tux dilemma. "He, uh . . . hasn't picked one out yet."

All the catalogs dropped to the floor. "You're joking," said Vesta, shocked.

Sabrina gave a weak chuckle. "Nope. I can't choose my dress until he chooses his tux. But it was really nice of you to stop by—"

"This is wonderful, Sabrina! *You* can set the

tone!" Vesta clapped her hands, and the catalogs leaped into the air again, opening to the right pages. "Oh, this is going to be so much more exciting. We'll have so many more styles to choose from!"

"We . . . ?"

"Here, what do you think of this one?" Vesta pointed at her, and suddenly Sabrina found herself wearing a multilayered floral chiffon dress, diamond earrings, a tiara that shone with the light of a real star, and sandals studded with jewels. "It's an original Louie Sans Nom, one of the top designers in the Other Realm."

Hilda and Zelda entered the room and immediately averted their eyes. "My, that's bright," Zelda said, wincing.

"Can you turn it down?" Hilda asked. "I think my retinas are burning."

"Too much?" Vesta pointed again, and the glaring outfit was replaced by a somber blood-red velvet pant suit. "Then what about this one? Very deep, very rich, very sophisticated." She zapped a full-length mirror in front of her niece. "What do you think, Sabrina?"

Sabrina was busy looking at the far corner of the living room, where her fledgling Fair Wind had gathered itself into a sickly yellow ball of fog. Slowly it faded away. *So much for that,* she thought, and glanced up—right into the mirror. "Whoa!" The velvet suit was beautiful, and it actually brought out reddish highlights in her blond hair that Sabrina never knew she had. *Wait a minute, that's coloring,* she realized. "No, Aunt Vesta, this is really pretty, but it's not me."

Vesta raised her hand to point again. "Then what about—"

"Hold it!" ordered Sabrina.

To her surprise, Vesta obeyed. "What's the matter, dear?"

"Aunt Vesta, I really appreciate what you're trying to do, but there are some circumstances involved in my dress choice that I can't really discuss. Even beyond that, I have things under control on my own." Sabrina headed for the staircase. "Look, I have to study for a test tomorrow. But I promise, I'll pick a dress real soon, okay?"

Vesta watched her disappear up the stairs. "Oh, the poor dear's nervous. I know just what she needs."

"To be left alone?" tried Hilda.

Vesta smiled. "Hardly. That would be the worst thing for her." With a snap of her fingers, Vesta gathered her catalogs back into a giant floating pile and headed up to the linen closet. "It's been such a thrill visiting you all," she said as she left. "Tell Sabrina to leave everything to me."

After she was gone, Hilda heaved a sigh. "Well, you know what I always say about a bad problem—maybe it'll simply go away. After all, Vesta did."

"But she was right about one thing," said Zelda. "Someone's got to help Sabrina."

"No, you heard what Sabrina said: she can choose her own dress, and I think she should. It's not our decision to make, and it's not Vesta's, either. Right?" Hilda said.

The two sisters looked hard at each other.

"Oh, you're right," Zelda finally said. "I won't interfere."

"And neither will I," said Hilda.

What Vesta would do, however, was anybody's guess.

The next morning Sabrina arrived at school to discover that the Fair Wind was still blowing through the halls. At first she panicked, realizing that by doubling spell she had prolonged its life beyond normal. But she was lured into the spirit of things when Mr. Kraft waved merrily at her, Libby gave her a cheerful hello, and the homeroom teachers provided doughnuts and milk before classes started. Fairness reigned, and it was great!

Only one thing still worried her: her aunts were planning to chaperon the prom. "The weird thing is, I didn't send them a letter," she told Valerie. "I was in charge of the mailing labels, and I distinctly remember taking their label off the list before giving it to you. Maybe that was a little underhanded, but I didn't want them to know about it. So I don't understand how a copy of the letter reached them."

"I delivered it," Valerie told her matter-offactly. "After all, Sabrina, it wouldn't be fair for the rest of us to have our parents at the prom and not you. I took a copy of the letter to your house yesterday after the committee meeting."

While I was running around campus trying to catch the Fair Wind, thought Sabrina. She started to get mad, then thought better of it. Obviously Valerie had acted under the influence of the Fair Wind. *Okay, maybe not everything is better when it's fair,* she thought. *This was my own fault, though, so I'll deal with it.*

Her first class was math, and there was going to be a test. Although she'd tried to study the night before, Sabrina hadn't been able to concentrate—especially when Salem had started mewling in his sleep. So now she hurried to the classroom and took the precious few minutes before the bell to cram.

Other kids started filing in, and when the noise level got too high, Sabrina gave up. "I will meet doom with a calm, serene heart," she said philosophically, closing her textbook.

Harvey, who sat a few desks away, gave her a thumbs-up. "That's the spirit, Sabrina. If you're doomed to fail, at least do it cheerfully. I certainly intend to."

The bell rang and Mrs. Quick entered the classroom, copies of the math test under her arm. "Good morning, class. As you know, we have our test today."

Everybody groaned.

"I hope you all studied because the test is a thorough one, though I don't think it's too hard, really." Mrs. Quick paused as a warm wind blew through the room, flinging a few papers off her desk. "My goodness, did someone leave the window open?"

Sabrina knew exactly what had happened, but she said nothing. Instead she crossed her fingers and hoped, *Maybe she'll call the test off because it's unfair.*

"Well, anyway," said Mrs. Quick, "I was saying that this shouldn't be too hard for any of you. But just to be fair, I'm going to make it an open-book test."

The students cheered. Sabrina shrugged. *Okay, I can handle that.*

"But only for the dumb students," Mrs. Quick continued. "They need all the help they can get. Smart students like Sabrina Spellman should be able to ace this test without their book. Is that all right with everybody?"

"What?" cried Sabrina. "Wait a minute—"

"Oh, you'll do fine, Sabrina." Mrs. Quick laid a copy of the test on Sabrina's desk. "I have faith in you." She passed out the rest of the tests, and all the other students eagerly opened their textbooks. Sabrina got to work, seething with the injustice of it. *After this class, I'm going to get that Fair Wind and stuff it back into its jar!* she promised herself.

* * *

Finding the Fair Wind was no big challenge.

After her math test, Sabrina stepped out into the hallway to see a crowd of students at the far end. Somebody began beating a drum, a pair of cymbals clashed, and the crowd parted to reveal Westbridge High School's two foremost nerds, Gordie and Trudy. Each of them held a bullhorn, and they took turns speaking as the telltale *whoosh* of the Fair Wind blew past.

"It's time for a revolution!" Gordie blared.

"It's time for Westbridge High to embody the spirit of true democracy and equality!" Trudy shrilled.

"It's time for *fair* leadership at Westbridge High!" they shouted in unison.

The crowd roared approval.

Sabrina gulped. "Uh-oh."

Chapter 10

"Electing Student Council members by popularity is unfair!" Trudy boomed over her bullhorn. "We call for new elections!"

"Fair elections!" added Gordie.

"Based on issues, not personalities!"

"Why wait till next year? We want democratic leadership now!"

The crowd started to chant and clap in rhythm. "Now! Now! Now! Now!"

Sabrina could only watch in horror. Gordie and Trudy were already on the Student Council—Gordie was treasurer and Trudy was secretary. These were considered geek positions, since the popular kids holding the rest of the council positions hated math and detested taking notes. Gordie and Trudy had always been meek and mild, but now they were full-blown crusaders. Their lung power astonished Sabrina, who had never before heard bashful little Trudy speak above a whisper.

Suddenly Sabrina felt the Fair Wind blow past—much stronger now and almost visible in its roiling yellowness. She held her skirt down as Harvey raised his right arm, fist clenched. "New elections!" he roared.

"Ouch!" Sabrina said. "Please don't shout in my ear!"

"Sorry." Harvey bounded off to join the crowd, shouting, "Now! Now! Now! Now!"

"I've created a monster," Sabrina muttered. "I've got to stop this." She reached into her pocket, only then remembering that the glass jar was in her locker. "Oh, great." She waved wildly at the crowd. "Hey, everybody? Don't do anything stupid until I get back, okay?"

They weren't listening to her, they were listening to Gordie, who was outlining his and Trudy's election platform. Sabrina could hear his voice echo down the hall as she dashed to her locker. "Our first issue will be bathroom use," Gordie blared. "It's only fair that girls get more bathrooms than boys. There's never a line at the boys' bathroom, but always at the girls'."

Trudy lifted her bullhorn and added, "Next, nerd girls get their own sink-and-mirror areas so that we're free from the cheerleaders who primp so long we never get a chance to wash our hands."

The crowd roared its approval.

"Nerds and geeks should have their own area set aside in the cafeteria," Gordie declared. "We're sick of getting stuff spilled on us *by accident.*"

"And from here on, all students will treat nerds like popular kids."

"In fact, everybody will automatically be members of the Science Club!"

Again the crowd roared its approval. Sabrina fumbled her locker open and rooted around for the glass jar, thinking, *Those ideas may seem fair, but they're awfully extreme the other way.* But nobody was objecting. In fact, when she returned to the crowd, Sabrina found the cheerleaders in a line shouting,

> We want elections,
> New, fair elections!
> We want 'em now
> And we don't care how!

Everybody took up the cheer until the hallway P.A. system crackled to life. "Attention, students," came Mr. Kraft's voice. "Attention all students."

The shouting died down.

Mr. Kraft continued: "Being a fair and honest man, Principal LaRue has decided to allow emergency elections for a new Student Council. Gordie will be on the ballot for Student Council president, and Trudy will be on the ballot for vice-president. Anybody else who stands for fairness and equality, please step forward!"

Everybody in the hall took a step forward. When they realized what they'd done, they all started laughing.

"Elections will be held next Friday," Kraft's voice said, and the P.A. system fell silent.

As the students started to cheer again, Sabrina held her glass jar open and silently summoned the Fair Wind. Nothing. *Come on, you stupid wind, I made you! Get over here!*

Nothing.

Several football players lifted Gordie and Trudy up on their shoulders and carried them down the hall amid clapping and cheering. Sabrina could see a vague yellow mass blow through the crowd one way and then the other. Nobody noticed when their hair got ruffled or their skirts billowed. Sabrina tried again to summon the wind, even pointing her finger right at it, but nothing happened. As if it now had a mind of its own, the Fair Wind ignored her.

Harvey was following the crowd when a voice stopped him in his tracks. "Kinkle!" It was the wrestling coach, who looked Harvey in the eye and said, "Kinkle, I've decided to put you on the team. It's only fair, since you worked so hard for the tryouts. I'll expect you at practice tomorrow."

Harvey beamed with pleasure. "Yes, sir!" He

turned to Sabrina. "Wow, did you hear that, Sabrina?"

"Oh, yeah," Sabrina said, wondering if the news was really that good. Harvey liked wrestling, but the truth was, he wasn't very good at it. *He's going to get pummeled!* she thought.

Valerie ran up to her, smiling so hard that Sabrina thought her face might crack. "Sabrina, you'll never guess what happened! Libby just asked me to be on the *first-string* cheerleading squad! Can you believe it? That must mean she really likes me! I'm finally going to be in with the popular crowd!" She lowered her voice. "But we can still be friends, right?"

Sabrina just nodded. "Sure."

"Oh, good." Valerie gave her a hug just as the other cheerleaders dashed up, breathless with all the excitement.

"Valerie, it's time to practice the new cheer," Cee Cee said.

"The first string—*just* the first string—will be cheering after school today during the Chess Club competitions," said Libby.

Valerie looked like she was going to faint. "This is like a dream come true!"

Sabrina cocked her head. "The *Chess Club* competition?"

"That's what I said," Libby affirmed. "After all, it's only fair that we cheerleaders support all school activities, not just the athletes, right?"

"And I wrote the new cheer," said ditzy Cheri. "Wanna hear it? Ready, and—

Castles, pawns, and horsie-things,
Pointy-pieces, queens and kings,
Get those markers on that board,
Hop those squares and score, score, score!
Gooooooooo team!

The cheerleaders applauded. "Excellent," said Libby. "C'mon, girls." They all scampered off, including Valerie.

Within moments, the hallway was empty. Stranger yet, it was quiet. Sabrina stood there, stunned. "Oh, boy, I'm in trouble."

Doubling the Fair Wind had been a bad idea. True, Libby now behaved with more consideration for others than Sabrina would ever have thought possible, but the rest of the school was going nuts before her very eyes.

She zapped herself home to consult her magic book. Only when she carefully read the Fair Wind spell instructions again did she notice the fine print at the bottom of the page. It read: "Do not alter ingredients. Do not augment the potion. Do not keep more than one week." And in red letters it said, *"Warning:* Do not use doubling spell to hasten effect."

She turned to Salem, who was sitting on her

desk licking his belly fur. "Why didn't you tell me it said this?" she demanded.

Salem looked up in mid-lick, his tongue still sticking out of his mouth. "Whath you thay?"

"You said you sneaked in and watched me make the Fair Wind potion. Why didn't you tell me about these warnings?"

Salem sucked his tongue back into his mouth. "Excuse me, but even I can't read fine print from across a room. Pray tell, why didn't *you* notice the warnings? This isn't exactly the first time you've made that mistake. Some witch you're going to make, always saying 'Oops!' after each spell."

"Okay, okay, so I'm lazy and I didn't read the whole page!" Sabrina snarled in frustration. "But now what am I going to do?"

"You'll have to summon the Fair Wind back."

"I can't. It won't listen to me anymore."

Salem shook his head. "Not good. Once you lose control over a wind, it's kind of hard to catch. I guess you'll just have to wait until it blows itself out."

"And how long will that take?"

"Since you doubled its strength, which actually quintuples a Fair Wind potion, I'd say it'll blow around campus for another week or so."

"Another *week?*" Sabrina's knees buckled. Fortunately, a chair was behind her and she landed neatly in it. "I can't wait another week. The prom is this Saturday. Parents will be there." Her heart skipped a beat. "Omigosh, Aunt Hilda and Aunt Zelda will be there! I can't let them be affected by the Fair Wind! Once they find out I made this potion, they'll kill me!"

"And they'll think it's fair to kill you, too," Salem pointed out. "I'd say you've got a problem."

Sabrina glared at the cat. "I hate it when you say that.'"

"Then let me say this—have you ever heard of a Twist-Back potion?"

Sabrina searched her memory. "No."

"It's a little thing we witches can do when a potion goes awry. If there's no other way to fix it, you brew up a Twist-Back potion—that is, you make the potion again, but you use the opposite of all the ingredients. The object is to twist the potion back onto itself to cancel it."

Sabrina didn't like the sound of that. "Are you sure that's a legal procedure?"

Salem's ears flattened. "Hey, I'm the guy who tried to take over the world. Don't ask me about legal. Just ask me if it works."

"Does it work?"

"I dunno, I've never heard of anybody who had the guts to try it."

Sabrina perused the list of Fair Wind potion ingredients. "Well, I've got no choice. One Twist-Back potion comin' up!"

☆

Chapter 11

☆

The next morning Sabrina arrived at school an hour early to release her Twist-Back potion. It hadn't been difficult to make, but it had taken almost all night to ferment, just as the original Fair Wind potion had done. Now she held in her hands a glass jar that was filled with a roiling *purple* cloud. Turning the lid, she chanted an activation spell that would send the new wind after the original Fair Wind:

Wherever you are, whatever you do
This Twist-Back potion's the end of you.

She lifted the lid.

The Twist-Back Wind zoomed out the jar and around the empty hallway like a purple phantom, then dissipated, but not so completely that Sabrina couldn't still see it. She followed it down another hallway, up the stairs and around the corner.

A warm breeze blew by. *It's the Fair Wind! Go get it, Twist-Back!*

The two winds met, and the Fair Wind flared brilliant yellow while the Twist-Back Wind flared purple. Rainbow lightning flashed, and the hallway shook with thunder. Not expecting such a violent reaction, Sabrina almost got knocked off her feet. *I hope the janitor's not around. He'll think the school's under alien attack!* she thought, leaning back and steadying herself against some lockers.

The two winds floated around and through each other like foggy wrestlers trying to get a grip on a slippery opponent. Sparks of magic shot out in all directions wherever they touched, and Sabrina began to wonder if her Twist-Back potion would win. The original Fair Wind seemed to be brighter and more powerful than ever.

Suddenly a mouth formed in the Fair Wind's foggy yellow depths. The mouth opened wide and swallowed up the purple Twist-Back Wind in a single gulp. With an audible belch, the Fair Wind's yellow color faded and the cloud became an odd combination of pale yellow and purple stripes. Sabrina could actually see the wind blow past, and it felt warmer and stronger than before.

She flapped her hands in the air, a pointless gesture motivated by sheer helplessness. "The whole thing's backfired! I've got to stop it!" she cried, and booked after it.

Twenty minutes later Sabrina was sitting alone in the empty school cafeteria, nursing a soda she had bought from a vending machine. The Fair Wind had eluded her. She didn't want to admit that she would have had no idea what to do with it if she'd caught it—at the time, the chase was the thing. Now she was just trying to catch her breath and devise a strategy. Unfortunately, it was nearly time for school to start. Students were arriving, and as they did, the chances for more mayhem increased.

With a heavy sigh, Sabrina hauled herself to her feet and trudged to her locker. She'd hardly gotten it open when Harvey arrived, his right arm cradled in a sling. "Harvey, what happened?" she asked in alarm.

"I got hurt," he told her in his simple, straight forward way.

"I can see that," Sabrina said, following him to his locker. "But how? Don't tell me it happened at wrestling practice."

Since Harvey's good arm was carrying books, he grasped his locker handle in his teeth, lifted it up, then bumped the locker door open with his head. "It did, but not because of wrestling," he explained. "All the guys on the team congratulated me for making it in. They slapped me on the shoulder a lot. I think it got dislocated."

Sabrina didn't know what to say, but fortunately she was spared the need to figure something out. Valerie skipped up to her, dressed in her green-and-white cheerleader outfit complete with pom-poms. "Two, four, six, eight, who do we appreciate?" she cheered. "Everybody! Yaaaaay!"

"Hi, Val," Sabrina said, trying not to feel betrayed by the sight of her best friend wearing the enemy's official costume. She doubted she'd ever really get used to it.

"Hi, hello, how are you? Westbridge spirit is here for you! Yaaaaaay!"

Sabrina had never seen Valerie so happy before. "You look good, Val, honest. You'll make a great first string cheerleader."

Leaping and shaking her pom-poms, Valerie cried out, "Glad you think so. Yes, I do! Let me do a cheer for you! Spellman, Spellman, rah-rah-rah!"

"Okay, enough already. Can you stop jumping around so I can talk to you for a minute?"

"Sorry, sorry, no can do! There's no time to talk to you! I must practice cheers and stuff, 'cause this gig is really tough!" And away she leaped, shaking her pom-poms and rah-rahing her way down the hall.

"Great. I've created a rhyme addict." Sabrina moped. "I can't believe this. There must be something I can do!"

"There most certainly is something you can do," said Mrs. Reilly, striding up to her. "You can take that sign off Harris's back."

Sabrina looked where her English teacher was pointing and saw that somebody had taped a Kick Me sign on William Harris, one of the more obnoxious kids in school. Sabrina pulled it off without Harris's noticing and started to crumple it up when Mrs. Reilly stopped her. "No, no, no, put it on *me.*" She turned around, offering her back to Sabrina. "If Harris has to suffer, it's only fair that I should suffer, too."

"Mrs. Reilly, I really don't think that's—"

"Don't argue, please. Just tape it on."

Sabrina obeyed, wondering if anybody would really have the guts to kick the English teacher. *I guess it would only be fair,* she thought, but dared not say it aloud.

Mrs. Reilly reached around to make sure the sign was in place. "Thank you, Sabrina. I feel much better now."

As Harvey watched the teacher walk away with the Kick Me sign stuck to her back, he bobbed his head in admiration. "That, Sabrina, is a great woman."

"A great loon, you mean."

"What?"

"Oh, never m—" Sabrina stopped short as somebody yelped. She whirled around to witness an amazing sight: one by one, students' belongings were being blown right out of their hands. Books hit the ceiling, papers scattered everywhere, and purses, combs, wallets, and hats sailed out of reach. "It's the Fair Wind!" Sabrina gasped, seeing the faint outline of a yellow-and-purple haze weave its way through the crowd. "It's definitely not fair anymore—it's gone honkers!"

"Who are you talking to, Sabrina?" Harvey asked pleasantly.

Sabrina clutched at her own hair. "My invisible friend!" she blurted, and took off full tilt after the Fair Wind—or rather, in the direction that the Fair Wind was going. *There must be some way to get rid of it before Westbridge High ends up on an episode of* Unexplained Phenomena! she thought wildly.

Then an idea hit her. Her magic book had said that the Fair Wind affected only those people who entered its sphere of influence. In other words, since the Fair Wind had been released inside the school, that was the only place it could operate. *So all I have to do is blow it out a window!*

Slowing her pace, she zapped a big fan into her hands, then ducked around a corner to await the wind's return. Barely was she in place when it came back, perhaps curious as to why she'd stopped chasing it. Peeking around the corner, Sabrina saw the faint yellow-and-purple haze hovering about ten feet away. She knew that not far beyond the haze was a door leading out to the quad, so she gripped the fan tightly, one finger poised on the power switch. *It's now or never, Sabrina!*

She leaped out of hiding and switched the fan on. *"En garde,* you stupid wind!" she yelled.

Nothing happened. She'd forgotten to plug the fan in!

Uttering a growl of pure frustration, Sabrina pointed at the fan. One quick spark of magic, and the fan instantly began to operate sans electricity. Sabrina leaped after the Fair Wind and began to blow it down the hallway, the unplugged electrical cord of the fan trailing after her like a long tail. "It's working!" she told Harvey as she raced past him, heading for the door. "Somebody open the door!"

A student obligingly swung the door open, and Sabrina clicked her fan to full speed, pushing the Fair Wind before her faster and faster. Just as it reached the door, however, it veered off to one side, leaving Sabrina to charge outside by herself.

"Get back here!" she growled, and ran back in after it.

For ten minutes Sabrina chased the Fair Wind around the school. She felt like a complete idiot, but nobody seemed to pay attention, which was good . . . though she couldn't understand why, which was bad. Regardless, the Fair Wind blew increasingly faster, while the teenage witch grew increasingly tired.

Finally she had to give up. She'd driven it straight at three doors and about seven windows, but each time, the darned thing had veered away. The last she saw of it, it was blasting its way down a corridor in the form of a small tornado.

Her arms were exhausted from holding up the

fan for so long, so Sabrina zapped it away and collapsed into a chair. "I give up. I'm resigned to finishing my education at Freaky Wind High School." She hardly took notice when the vending machine stock man ran past, his arms full of candy bars and cookie packs.

"It's all mine!" he was shouting hysterically. "It's not fair that everybody gets to eat it but me! It's mine now, all mine!" He nearly ran into Maria French, the richest girl in the school.

Normally Maria walked the halls like a high fashion model, wearing the latest clothing designs and looking stylishly bored with life. Now she stumbled toward Sabrina, tears streaming down her face in long mascara-smeared lines. "It's not fair! Everybody is poor except me! I want to be poor, too! I want to be poor, too!" She fell to her knees, sobbing like Scarlett O'Hara about Rhett Butler.

"Oh, get a grip," Sabrina snapped at her.

"What did you say?" came Mr. Kraft's voice, pitched high in surprise. Sabrina turned to find him speaking, not to her, but to Mrs. Quick.

"I said, I want to teach a music class," Mrs. Quick repeated.

"But you're a math teacher."

"Math is a lot like music. Or is it the other way around? Well, either way, I really like music and I want to teach it."

Mr. Kraft folded his arms. "Do you know

anything about music? Do you have your music certification? Can you even sing a scale?"

Mrs. Quick drew herself up to her full height. "No, but I'll fake it."

"I'm sorry, Mrs. Quick, but—"

"Unfair!" Mrs. Quick bellowed, cutting him off. "I'm being persecuted by the vice-principal!" She started marching down the hall, waving her fists in the air. "I want to teach music, and Mr. Kraft won't let me! Unfair! Unfair!"

Kraft's face turned beet red. "Hey, you can't say that!" he cried out, and marched down the hallway after her. "Don't listen to her! She can't say those things about me! They may be true, but it's still unfair!"

Just when she thought things couldn't get any weirder, Sabrina heard the sound of drums and cymbals. Gordie and Trudy were on the warpath again, heading toward her, surrounded by a throng of student supporters who clapped and hooted. "New elections!" they were chanting. "New elections!"

"You already got permission to hold new elections!" Sabrina shouted over the din.

The drumming and hooting stopped. "We're not talking about the Student Council anymore," Gordie said, the light of power mania shining in his eyes. "The Student Council is just a puppet organization, a sham, a joke. The real power lies with school administration."

"I'm running for principal," declared Trudy.

"And I'm running for vice-principal," said Gordie.

"And I'm vouching for them," came a new voice.

Sabrina's jaw dropped. "Principal LaRue?"

The Westbridge High School principal stepped forward, a pair of shining brass cymbals in his hands. "These kids are ready for the responsibility, and frankly, I'm pooped. It's only fair they take over running this school. Come on, kids, let's campaign!" He banged his cymbals so loud that Sabrina winced.

The drummer started drumming again, and the throng of students around Gordie and Trudy resumed hooting and cheering.

"Okay, this has gone far enough." Sabrina ran for the pay phones, digging in her pockets for a quarter. "I don't care what Aunt Zelda and Aunt Hilda do to me, I've got to get their help." She had barely started to punch in her home phone number when a puff of smoke erupted in the hall.

It cleared to reveal Aunt Vesta, dressed in a cherry-red leather miniskirt and a billowing white silk blouse. Her long, shapely legs sparkled from the glitter on her pantyhose, and the heels on her shoes were so high that she was almost standing on her toes. She lifted her Gucci sunglasses and batted the long lashes of her gorgeous blue eyes.

"Hello, Sabrina dear. I'm so glad I found you." She glanced around. "I'd forgotten how drab your little school is."

"Drab, maybe," said Sabrina. "Dull, never. Aunt Vesta, what are you doing here?"

"Surprise! Your auntie Vesta is taking you shopping." And with a radiant smile and a flourish of one perfectly manicured finger, Vesta and Sabrina disappeared.

☆

Chapter 12

☆

Sabrina found herself in a shopping mall so large that she couldn't see either end of it, nor could she see the ceiling, which she presumed must be high above her somewhere. Muted voices drifted by from all directions, and high-fashion shoppers strode past as bulging bags and boxes floated obediently behind them. "Where are we?" Sabrina demanded.

Vesta stood beside her. She had taken off her sunglasses and was tucking them into the white beaded purse that hung from her shoulder. "Le Paquet de Monnaie Mall, only the most fashionable shopping place in the Other Realm. I wouldn't dream of buying clothes anywhere else." She leaned over and whispered into Sabrina's ear, "Word of advice—you shouldn't either."

"Okay, we're in a mall," said Sabrina. "Next question: *why?*"

Vesta laid an arm across her niece's shoulders. "Because, dear Sabrina, I'm going to take you to the premier dress shop in either realm, and there I intend to buy you a proper outfit for your prom. I simply can't stand watching you struggle with indecision anymore."

Sabrina tried to remain calm. "Aunt Vesta, didn't you see the chaos at my school? I don't have time to shop right now!"

"Nonsense," Vesta declared. "No time for shopping? What a ridiculous notion."

"It's not a notion. It's my friends—"

"Who are only mortals. Whatever the problem is, your friends will survive till we're done. Now come with me." With her long legs aglitter, Vesta strode away, heading for a shop called the Best Drest.

The door opened automatically, and Sabrina felt herself being gently pulled through. *That's one way to suck in customers,* she thought.

An emaciated, sour-looking, long-faced, limp-haired model type slunk up to them and struck a moody mannequin pose. "May I help you?" she asked in a flat, uninterested voice.

"Yes, Vesta to see Mr. Drest personally," Vesta replied, her own tone so flat it rivaled the model type's. "Prom wear," and she waved vaguely at Sabrina.

The model type glanced at Sabrina, arched one

neatly plucked eyebrow, and waved her hand just the way Vesta had. On her, however, the movement looked almost too difficult. "This way, please."

"She seriously needs a cup of coffee," Sabrina whispered to Vesta.

"That's high fashion, dear," said Vesta curtly. "Enervation sells."

Sabrina followed her aunt deep into the store, past racks of clothing and shelves of shoes and mountains of makeup and countertops overflowing with jewelry and other accessories. "Wait here," said the model type. "Don't touch anything." She disappeared into a back room.

"Don't touch anything?" Sabrina asked. "How are you supposed to shop if you can't touch anything?"

"Only Drest touches the clothes," said Vesta, as if it should have been obvious. "You'll see how it works."

"Vesta my dear!" boomed a deep voice. A short, balding middle-aged male witch dressed in a smart pin-striped suit and wing-tip shoes hurried up to Vesta. His skin was so suntanned he could have passed for a large suitcase. Scooping up Vesta's hand, he kissed it, the rings and bracelets on his own hands shining and clinking in unison with hers. Vesta reacted to this greeting as if she were charmingly embarrassed, but Sabrina knew she had expected it all along.

"Drest, you cad! Why didn't you come to my

party? Greenland is a wonderful place once the temperature's controlled. I kept it at eighty-five degrees all weekend, but you never showed up."

An air of apology radiated from Drest's very pores. "Vesta, Vesta, Vesta, pearl of my heart, I despise Greenland. You know that."

To Sabrina, Vesta said, "Liar. He doesn't want to admit that he simply doesn't like the mortal realm."

"It's so mundane," Drest complained, then looked at Sabrina as if just noticing her presence. "And who is this?"

"This," said Vesta, glowing with pride, "is my little niece, Sabrina, and it's time for her first prom. We need a dress, Drest, and we need her dressed the best."

"I know just the thing." Drest stepped over to a clothes rack, pulled something out, and threw it at Sabrina.

"Hey!" Sabrina yelled, but Drest's magic instantly transformed the outfit on the hanger into a perfect size for Sabrina. The next thing she knew, she was wearing it. She had hardly realized that when she also realized that she could see herself as though she were looking into a mirror. It was as if the very air reflected her image.

"How you like, eh?" Drest prompted.

Sabrina was wearing a floor-length black satin gown. As she gawked at her reflection, her hair wove itself into a complicated braided bun topped by a diamond tiara. A matching necklace appeared around her neck. "Uhh . . ."

"She's speechless," Vesta said with amusement.

"No. It's beautiful, but it's just . . . not me," Sabrina said. "Look, Aunt Vesta—"

"Too black, right?" interrupted Drest. "Try this." He pulled another hanger from the rack and tossed it at her.

Now Sabrina was wearing a pink velvet minidress and jacket with marabou trim and matching pink leather ankle boots.

"She might prefer a cardigan sweater top with that," mused Drest, "maybe something with beads."

Sabrina's jacket became a cardigan sweater with an elaborate gold-and-silver bead design in a vine-and-leaf motif. Her hair unraveled from its ornate braid and frizzed itself into a medieval-style mane. "Aunt Vesta, please—" Sabrina tried again, but Vesta was too wrapped up with Drest now.

"Try Oriental," she suggested.

Drest rummaged through the rack, snatched up an outfit, and flung it at Sabrina. Now she wore a beautiful Chinese cheong-sam dress in vibrant red with an elaborately embroidered gold dragon down the right side. A long slit ran up the left side.

Drest eyed the creation critically. "One slit or two?" he asked Vesta.

"Two," decided Vesta. "Easier for dancing."

Instantly a second slit tore itself up the fabric next to Sabrina's right leg. "Whoa!" the teenager said as the embroidered dragon came to life, blowing smoke from its nostrils. It shifted its position to accommodate the new design feature. Then it settled back down and became lifeless embroidery again. "Aunt Vesta, I don't think a live dragon on my dress is Westbridge material."

"Maybe you're right," Vesta agreed. "Mortals have never understood dragons. I know!" She bent over and whispered into Drest's ear.

He smiled and nodded. "I know the one you mean." Going to a different clothes rack, Drest shuffled around for a moment, then pulled out a hanger and threw an outfit at Sabrina.

Now she was wearing a white-dyed leather halter top with matching leather jacket and pants with faux fox fur trim. Witch magic made the white leather shimmer with silvery highlights.

"If I may," Vesta said to Drest, and she pointed at Sabrina's hair, which instantly split into dozens of tight coils. "And I have just the finishing touch. A hair snake!"

"Hair snake?" Sabrina asked cautiously.

"They're marvelous," Drest assured her. "They tighten around your hair and change configuration throughout the evening, giving you a new look every, oh, twenty minutes or so. Simply smashing."

"A live snake?" Sabrina squealed. "In my hair? Don't you dare!"

"But it's the height of fashion, Sabrina," said Vesta. "Really, you're so squeamish."

"No, what I am is fed up." Sabrina pointed at herself, returning her own school outfit to her body. Both Drest and Vesta gasped in shock, but Sabrina tried to be cool about it. "Look, I'm done shopping, okay?"

Vesta relaxed. "Why didn't you just say so?" To Drest she said, "She'll take the white leather number, sans the hair snake. Don't worry, I'll have Enrique whip up an appropriate hairstyle for her."

A receipt pad and pen appeared in Drest's hands. "Fair enough." He started scribbling. "It will be ready for pickup in twelve hours."

That made no sense to Sabrina. "Why twelve hours? I was just wearing it."

"That was the rack model," explained Vesta. "You can't purchase the rack model; it's a Flexi-Fit, designed for try-ons only." She gave Drest an apologetic shrug. "She doesn't shop much, poor thing."

Drest patted her arm. "We'll fix that." He handed Vesta a receipt. "Charge to your regular account, my love? Excellent. Now then, I must go. I have a display appointment in the, uh"—he frowned—"mortal realm. Ta." Drest hurried back to his office.

"He's an artist," Vesta purred. "Oh, and, Sabrina—be a dear and don't tell Zelda or Hilda about this, hm? I want it to be a surprise."

"It'll be a surprise, all right," Sabrina said, and marched for the exit. She had no intention of wearing the chosen outfit, but if Vesta insisted on buying it for her, she wouldn't bother arguing. All she wanted to do right now was get back to Westbridge and stop the Not-So-Fair Wind.

But Vesta wasn't finished. "On to accessories," she said, catching up to Sabrina and maneuvering her to the nearest cosmetics counter.

"But, Aunt Vesta—"

"Tut-tut!" Vesta said sharply. "On prom night, there are certain things a girl must have." She picked up a bottle of nail polish. "This is mood polish. It will change color—"

"According to my mood," Sabrina finished impatiently. "We have that kind of thing in the mortal realm, Aunt Vesta. It doesn't work."

"This does," Vesta said. "And for your information, it doesn't monitor *your* moods, it monitors the moods of the people around you. That way, you can act accordingly. Blending in is the secret to social success, after all." She placed the polish in a small shopping basket. "Oh, and you must have one of these." It was a powder compact.

"I've got one," said Sabrina. "In fact, I've got several."

"Not like this." Vesta opened it up, and Sabrina heard a stadium-size crowd cheering. Tiny pieces of confetti flew out of the powder section, and several tiny hands reached out from the little mirror and waved. Vesta basked in the adoration, then snapped the compact shut and dropped it into her shopping basket. "Remember when I showed you my Hall of Gratuitious Praise? This is the pocketbook version. Every woman should have one. A dose of adulation does wonders for one's confidence."

"Not to mention one's ego," Sabrina mumbled.

"Ah, here it is." Vesta snatched up a can of glitter paint. "For your hair. If you're not going to use a snake, at least you want your tresses to match your outfit. Oh, and here's the final touch"—reverently she picked it up—"a Cinderella watch."

Sabrina's lip curled. "Isn't that a little young for me?"

Vesta held it up to show her a normal watch face that bore no picture of Cinderella or anything else to do with the fairy tale.

"So why call it a Cinderella watch if she's not on it?" Sabrina asked, puzzled.

"Because if you set it correctly, your date will turn into a pumpkin at midnight."

Sabrina was horrified. "I don't want Harvey to turn into a pumpkin!"

"You want to keep track of the time, don't you?"

"Not that way!" Once again Sabrina headed for the door. "Thank you, but I really have to get back to school." And she ran out of the Best Drest without another word. She could only hope that Vesta understood. *If I don't get back to school soon, there may not be a school for me to get back to!* she thought frantically.

First she stopped by the Spellman house. She really needed help from her other two aunts.

"Sabrina, there you are," Hilda said, emerging from the living room as Sabrina ran down the stairs. "I've been waiting for you to get home from school. We have to do this quickly, while Zelda's out."

"What do we have to do quickly?" asked Sabrina, reaching the landing. She stopped dead in her tracks as Hilda directed her gaze into the living room.

"Surprise!" said Hilda.

☆

Chapter 13

☆

The living room was crammed with clothing racks—very familiar clothing racks. And in the midst of them stood Mr. Drest. He gave a start, obviously not expecting to see Sabrina again. *So he had a display appointment in the mortal realm, eh?* Sabrina thought.

Hilda giggled with delight. "Sabrina, I'm going to buy you a prom outfit that will dazzle your peers. Mr. Drest, this is Sabrina, my niece. Sabrina, this is Sebastian Drest."

Drest opened his mouth as if about to say something like "We've met." Sabrina gave him a small but definite headshake, and Drest paused. "I am so very charmed to meet you," he finally said.

Acting as if she'd never seen Drest before, Sabrina said, "Hi. So, are you a local tailor?"

Drest bristled. Hilda said quickly, "Sabrina! This is no mortal tailor. Mr. Drest is the foremost designer in the Other Realm. He's the best of the best. Even your aunt Vesta buys from him."

Sabrina feigned surprise. "Really?"

Drest adjusted his impeccably tailored jacket. "Only the best buy from Drest."

"Hey, that would make a good motto."

"It's not a motto," Hilda said quietly in Sabrina's ear. "It's the truth. He costs a fortune, but I can't stand watching Vesta badger you. You deserve to pick out your own dress, and it should be the best."

Sabrina didn't know what to say. Since Hilda was grounded and couldn't leave the Spellman house, she'd obviously hired Drest to bring nearly half of his stock to her. But no matter how sweet a gesture it was, Sabrina still didn't have time to shop, not while the Fair Wind was making mincemeat of Westbridge High!

Hilda broke through Sabrina's dismal train of thought. "Okay, enough dawdling. Zelda will kill me if she sees me interfering, so let's accomplish this before she gets back. Sabrina, start shopping!"

"But, Aunt Hilda—"

"What would the young lady prefer?" asked Drest, contributing to Sabrina's dilemma as revenge for her "local tailor" insult. "How about something flowing?" Drest snatched an outfit from a nearby rack and threw it at Sabrina.

"Ooo, nice," Hilda commented as Sabrina suddenly wore a chiffon dress in dazzling fuchsia. "What about shoes?"

Drest pointed, and Sabrina's sneakers became elegant golden sandals.

"What do you think, Sabrina?" Hilda asked. When Sabrina just stood there looking frustrated, Hilda said, "Right. Too froufrou. Let's go for something with more oomph."

Drest flung another outfit at her, and Sabrina wore an elegant metallic silver satin pant suit and jacket.

Hilda whistled. "Definitely babe material."

Her brain awhirl with conflicting emotions, Sabrina blurted, "Aunt Hilda, please understand, I can't do this—"

"Oh, of course you can." Hilda put a comforting arm around Sabrina's shoulders. "Look, this is my gift to you, okay? Enjoy it. Don't worry about the cost. I want your prom to be the best." She frowned. "And I want you to have better memories than I do of my first dance." Unaffected by Drest's audible sigh of impatience, Hilda began her story. "My first dance, as you know, was a disaster. I keep telling Zelda that it was all Drell's fault. See, he and I were dating back then, and he presumed we'd be elected king and queen of the dance. When we didn't win, he got mad and turned some of the partygoers into turkeys—and then he plucked them in front of the rest of the gathering."

This wasn't quite what Sabrina had expected to hear. "Jeez, he didn't hurt them, did he?"

"Of course not, but they were incredibly embarrassed, and they had the most ridiculous bumpy-looking skin for weeks, even after they got their regular bodies back. When Daddy found out, he had a fit. No surprise there. I told him I'd had nothing to do with it, but I hadn't tried to stop Drell, either." Guilt crept into Hilda's voice as she confessed, "I was mad, you see. So I got grounded big time. You know the rest."

"I'm sorry you're still grounded," Sabrina said, "but I've got a little problem of my own, and if I don't solve it soon, I'll be worse than grounded."

Hilda's eyes narrowed. "What do you mean?"

Realizing she'd "oopsed," Sabrina tried to cover it with a laugh. "What? Oh, nothing. Never mind, honest. But I do have to go, Aunt Hilda, really. I'll come back as soon as I can." Sabrina felt rotten about leaving, but she had no choice. As Hilda eyed her with suspicion, she zapped her own clothes back on her body and hurried to the front door. "Nice to meet you, Mr. Drest. Goodbye!"

After she'd gone, Hilda turned to Drest and shrugged. "She'll take the pant suit."

Drest whipped out his receipt pad. "It will be ready for pickup in twelve hours."

* * *

Outside, Sabrina realized she didn't have time to get to school the mortal way. She was about to zap herself there when Zelda's car turned into the driveway. "Sabrina," Zelda called out the window. "What perfect timing. I need to see you."

"Sorry, Aunt Zelda, I'm in a rush—"

"Stop!"

Sabrina had been about to zap herself away, but something forced her pointing finger down. "Huh?"

"Don't be so eager to get to the Slicery to hang out with your friends," Zelda said, getting out of the car. "You've got to come with me first. I've got a surprise for you."

One zap, and Sabrina found herself standing in the Best Drest shop again. "Oh, no!"

Zelda looked hurt. "What do you mean, 'Oh, no'?" She softened. "Sweetie, I can't stand watching you get pushed around by Vesta. She means well and I love her dearly, but she can really be a pain in the behind. I just want you to be happy and enjoy your prom, so I've decided to buy you a dress. You pick out whatever you like."

Summoning the cooperation of every cheerful atom in her body, Sabrina gave Zelda a big smile. "Wow, that's so nice, Aunt Zelda."

"Just do me one little favor," Zelda said as an afterthought. "Don't tell Hilda or Vesta. I want this to be a surprise."

"Oh, it will be," Sabrina assured her.

Zelda beamed with pleasure and gestured to the store around them. "The Best Drest is supposed to be the finest clothing shop in the Other Realm, and since your aunt Vesta shops here, I can only presume that's true. Come on, let's take a look around."

"Welcome to the Best Drest," came a dour voice.

Sabrina whirled to find herself face to face with the emaciated, sour-looking, long-faced, limp-haired model-type store assistant. Sabrina's heart skipped a beat, but the assistant didn't seem to recognize her. *Not enough brain cells to support a memory,* Sabrina thought as the model type struck her moody mannequin pose. "May I help you?"

Zelda stepped forward. "Yes, thank you. I've made an appointment to see Mr. Drest. We've arrived a bit early, however."

The assistant lifted her scarecrow arm and consulted the gold watch strapped to her bony wrist. "He should be back in a few minutes. May I assist you until then?"

"No," Sabrina cut in. "No, thanks, we'll just browse and wait. Good-bye."

Zelda gave her a curious look as the model-type sashayed away.

"Sabrina, is something wrong?" Zelda asked.

"Wrong?" *An interesting question,* the teenage witch thought. *Things aren't* wrong *so much as they're bizarre, completely out of control, and getting worse all the time.* "No, nothing's wrong, Aunt Zelda. Why?"

"You seem tense, that's all. Never mind." Zelda flipped through clothes on the nearest rack. "What lovely things. Do you have any ideas about what you'd like to wear?"

"Ideas?" *I already have two outfits, neither of which will remotely coordinate with the disaster Harvey's going to be wearing!* "I haven't a clue," she said.

"Good afternoon," came an all too familiar voice. "May I help . . . ?" Sebastian Drest stopped dead and stared at Sabrina.

She bugged her eyes at him and gave a curt little shake of her head.

"You lovely ladies?" Drest finished. He gallantly scooped up Zelda's hand and kissed it. "Welcome to the Best Drest. You must be Zelda. I am always delighted to meet relatives of the lovely Vesta, one of my most charming customers. In fact, she was just here—"

Sabrina glared.

"Last week."

Zelda was blushing. "Vesta has spoken so highly of your shop that I've brought my niece, Sabrina, here to purchase a dress for her very first prom."

Drest tried not to look amused. "Is that so?"

"Yes, that's so," said Sabrina. "Show me something . . . different."

"Actually," Zelda said, "I was wondering about

a tux. Don't you think that would be cute, Sabrina?"

"A tux for the young lady?" Drest plucked an outfit from a rack and threw it at Sabrina.

Instantly she was dressed in white tie and tails. The white shirt sported a ruff and frilled sleeves, and the swallowtail cutaway and the slacks bore shiny satin trim. Her hair slicked itself back in a unisex style, and a white bow tie settled comfortably around her neck. "Oh, Sabrina, that looks absolutely fabulous," Zelda remarked.

As she had with Vesta, Sabrina could see herself reflected in an invisible mirror. The tux really did look good on her. "Okay, I'll take it!" Zapping her regular school clothes back on, Sabrina gave her startled aunt a hug. "Thank you so much, Aunt Zelda. It's beautiful and I can't wait to wear it, but I've gotta go now. Bye!" And she ran out the door.

Zelda turned to Drest. "Please excuse my niece's behavior. She does have good manners when she's not so excited."

Drest merely nodded with sage understanding. "Youth. What can you do with them?" he added philosophically. "Now, will that be cash or charge?"

Zelda blinked. "Oh. Charge."

"Fine," said Drest, scribbling in his receipt book. "The outfit will be ready in twelve hours."

* * *

A swirl of golden sparkles erupted in a hallway of Westbridge High School, and Sabrina appeared. The place was silent and empty. *Whatever happened, I missed it,* she thought. A quick tour of the halls convinced her that no horrible accidents had occurred, nor had any damage been done. She could only conclude that the Fair Wind had finally blown itself out.

Relieved, she zapped herself directly to her bedroom at home. "One problem down, one to go," she said: "What am I going to do with three prom dresses?"

Normally she would have discussed her dilemma with Salem, but he was in the Other Realm doing community service. Since he'd refused to choose a task, the Witches' Council had chosen for him—the poor cat was now an official patrolman at Dog Park, a canine recreation area in the Other Realm. He wouldn't be home till that evening, and with any luck, he'd come home in one piece.

Without Salem as her sounding board, Sabrina moped in silence. *What can I do?* she kept thinking. *What can I do?*

That was when her magic book moved all by itself on its wooden stand. It twitched. Then it jumped. Then its leather cover blew open, and the book flipped open to page after page until the riffling stopped at the picture of Sabrina's father. As portrayed in the black-and-white pencil sketch, he was a dapper young fellow in a turn-of-thecentury suit and top hat. As Sabrina looked on, the sketch came to life, and Edward Spellman turned to look out at his daughter. "Hello, Sabrina."

Books opening themselves and pictures coming to life normally didn't startle Sabrina anymore. Ever since her sixteenth birthday when she'd discovered she was a witch, bizarre occurrences had become commonplace. But this visitation was special—Edward Spellman, busy at a job in the Other Realm, didn't visit his daughter often. Sabrina wasn't only surprised; she was delighted to see him. "Daddy!"

"How's it going, honey?"

"Okay, I guess." Then Sabrina slumped. "Actually, not okay, I guess."

"I'm sorry to hear that, sweetie," her father said with feeling, "but I may have something to cheer you up." He bent over, apparently to pick up something, but in doing so, he disappeared below the frame of his picture. "I should have gotten this to you sooner," his disembodied voice continued, "but things have been a little hectic lately. Frankly I'm pleased I remembered at all." He straightened up and held a box out to her. It was large compared to his size, but tiny as far as Sabrina was concerned. "This is something your mother wanted you to have for your first prom, which, I believe, is going to take place tomorrow night, right?"

With a sinking feeling, Sabrina took the tiny box, which grew in size the moment it left the confines of the magic book. Sabrina set it on her bed and opened it. "Oh, dear," she said, gazing down at the pale peach taffeta gown, carefully folded in a thick bed of tissue paper. "It's a . . . dress."

Absolutely clueless as to her dilemma, Edward Spellman gave his daughter a grand smile. "Not just a dress, Sabrina—that's your mother's prom dress. She asked me to keep it preserved so that it would look perfect for you. Usually wedding dresses are handed down, but you know how our marriage ended up. Your mother figured this dress might pass on better memories."

Sabrina gulped, her eyes misting over. "Gee, Daddy . . . thanks."

If her father had had any notion that his daughter's tears were tears of frustration and not of joy, he would have reacted quite differently. As it was, he chuckled, pleased with himself. "I hope you haven't picked out a dress already. If you have, I guess this might pose a bit of a problem." He paused. "You haven't picked out a dress already, have you?"

Sabrina's answer was the awful truth. "No, I haven't."

"Oh, good. If you had, your mother would have killed me." A shrill beeping noise came from the picture, and Edward Spellman snatched a pager out of his vest pocket. "Gotta go, sweetheart. I love you. Have a wonderful prom! Bye!" He assumed the sideways pose of his original picture, and suddenly he *was* a picture again.

Sabrina closed her magic book and looked over at the dress in its box. *Eenie meeney miney moe?* she thought dismally.

☆

Chapter 14

☆

The next morning Sabrina got up, zapped herself into jeans and a T-shirt, sat down at her desk, put her chin in her hands, and thought. And thought. And thought. "There must be some way out of this," she repeated over and over, determined to find a solution.

Salem, who had arrived home from Dog Park patrol physically intact but mentally traumatized, spoke from under a pile of clothes in a corner, where he'd spent the entire night. "D-dogs," he stammered. "Dogs, everywhere. It was awful. I barely made it out alive!"

Sabrina had been listening to this kind of babbling all night, but at this point she couldn't feel sympathy for Salem anymore, especially since he'd admitted to teasing a schnauzer puppy with a fake bone. "I suppose I could use magic to combine all four dresses into one," she mused, "but I have a feeling that would be like mixing four colors of paint together. I'd end up with mush."

"The Great Danes and the mastiffs were bad enough," Salem's voice trembled from under the clothes pile, "but the toy poodles—they were the worst. All that yapping and yipping and drooling. And those cutesy little bows—I nearly went mad!"

"I could wear my mom's dress, but peach color next to Harvey's powder blue tux would make us look like a couple of Easter eggs. Besides, then my aunts would feel bad that I wasn't wearing their outfits."

"And the Chihuahuas, those wheezy little rodents—"

"If I could dye Mom's dress I'd stand a chance, but I don't know anything about taffeta. What if I ruin it?"

"And those ugly hot dog dogs—I *hate* dachshunds!"

Sabrina suddenly leaped out of her chair. "Wait a minute! I've got it!"

With a startled shriek, Salem leaped straight up from under the pile of clothes and landed on Sabrina's bed. Eyes bugged wide and claws fully out, he made a grand sweep of the room with one swift rotation of his head. "What—who—where?"

Sabrina wasn't listening. She grabbed up her mother's dress box and bounded out the door. "See ya, Salem!"

"Huh?" The cat watched her go, then sat down, disgusted. "That's the last time I look for sympathy in this house."

The Best Drest shop was always busy, but it was positively bustling with customers when Zelda entered. She patiently waited until an employee was free to help her.

"Welcome to the Best Drest, where you'll always be dressed the very best," said the emaciated, sour-looking, long-faced, limp-haired model-type store assistant. "May I help you?"

"Yes," said Zelda. "I'm here to pick up an outfit."

The model type indicated the back section of the store. "Please see Miss Cantrips at the pickup counter."

"Thank you." Zelda made her way to the back of the store where she found the last person she expected to see waiting at the pickup counter. "Oh, goodness me, look who's here—Vesta. What a surprise."

Vesta, sporting pink Capri pants, a yellow swimsuit top under a clear plastic jacket, and spike-heeled boots, turned around. For a split second, her lovely blue eyes registered shock when she saw her younger sister standing there.

Then she composed herself and flashed a brilliant smile. "Zelda. Darling. Whatever are you doing here?"

Zelda matched Vesta's stylishly casual air. "Shopping, naturally. And you?"

"Shopping, naturally." Vesta waited, as if expecting Zelda to leave. When Zelda didn't leave, she gestured at the pickup counter sign. "You've already ordered something, I see."

"What? Oh, yes," said Zelda, desperately wishing her sister would go elsewhere. "Just a little outfit. Nothing special. You?"

Vesta languidly waved a hand. "Another custom ensemble. You know how it is."

"Oh, yes, I certainly do."

The two sisters absently gazed around the store, each hoping the other would leave before Miss Cantrips showed up. What happened next surprised them both.

"What are you two doing here?" came a familiar voice.

Zelda and Vesta turned to see a small portable television set floating in the air. The person on the screen wasn't a TV star, however—it was Hilda.

"I thought you were grounded," Vesta said flatly.

"I am," replied Hilda. "But I checked the rules. I'm allowed to use a remote for emergencies."

"Such as?" prompted Zelda.

Hilda's TV image gave a hopeful little grin. "Shopping?"

Miss Cantrips chose that moment to approach them. "May I help you ladies?"

"Yes, I'm here to pick up an outfit for Sabrina Spellman," Zelda, Hilda, and Vesta all said at the same time.

Miss Cantrips paused. "Are you three suffering from a synchronicity spell, perhaps?" she inquired curiously.

The sisters glared at one another. "No," Zelda finally said, "but we are suffering from mutual interference in someone else's business. Am I right?"

Hilda's TV image slowly held up a hand. "Guilty as charged."

Vesta shrugged. "Guilty. So what of it?"

"What of it?" said Zelda. "Look, we all love Sabrina, but this isn't helping her. The poor thing must be in a frenzy of indecision by now, thanks to us."

"Excuse me, but was that name Sabrina Spellman?" asked Miss Cantrips.

The sisters nodded.

"She already picked up her order an hour ago."

The sisters traded looks of confusion. "She did?" they chorused.

Miss Cantrips nodded.

"She must have ordered her own dress behind my back," Vesta huffed. "Of all the nerve!"

"And after all the work I went through getting Drest to bring his inventory to the house," Hilda complained.

Zelda thought back to Sabrina's reaction when she'd entered the Best Drest shop. "No wonder she said 'Oh, no.'"

"Wait a minute." Hilda's TV monitor floated to the counter and set itself down. "Why are we all so upset? Sabrina obviously handled her own business the way she should have from the start, right? It's not our place to be angry with her. We should be angry at ourselves."

"Hilda's right," said Zelda. "Rather than help Sabrina, we all tried to influence her decision with our own preferences. It wasn't fair of us to put her through that."

"I suppose not," Vesta said reluctantly. "So what do we do now?"

"Nothing," said Zelda. "We've interfered enough. Sabrina's got her dress, so let's let her wear it to her prom."

"And I move we don't chaperon the prom, either," added Hilda.

Vesta's eyes lit up. "Chaperon? We can chaperon the prom? What a delightful idea!"

"No, Vesta," Zelda declared. "No more interference from any of us. Agreed?"

Hilda's TV image nodded solemnly. "Agreed."

Zelda turned to Vesta. "Agreed, Vesta?"

"But . . ." Vesta pursed her lips in defeat. "Oh, you're no fun."

The sisters parted company. Vesta went off to find something soothing to buy, Zelda zapped herself back to the mortal realm, and Hilda's TV image turned to static.

Chapter 15

☆

Saturday night. Almost six o'clock. The big evening was about to begin!

Sabrina stood before the mirror in her bedroom and checked her outfit one last time. She had spent the whole day putting it together, and now it was finally finished. "I think I'm ready," she said. "How do I look?"

Salem glanced up from the magazine he was reading. "No doubt about it," he said. "You look spiff."

"For once, cat, I'm inclined to agree with you." Sabrina winked at him and headed downstairs. "But I still have one last thing to do. I've got to put on nail polish before Harvey gets here."

In honor of Vesta, she'd already chosen a shade of mood nail polish that matched her dress. Fortunately, the polish dried instantly, since it was magical, so when the doorbell rang, she hurried to answer it without a thought of messing up her nails.

Harvey stood on the front porch, a vision in powder blue polyester. He almost dropped the corsage when he saw Sabrina. "Whoa!"

Sabrina twirled around to show off her mother's dress, which she'd taken to the Best Drest that morning to have dyed and modified to complement Harvey's dated tuxedo. It had been a magical rush order, but the extra cost had been worth it. Harvey's expression alone was worth it. "So what do you think?" she asked him. "Are we ready for *Saturday Night Fever* or what?"

"Whoa" was all Harvey could say again. Then he swallowed, with considerable effort. "You're the only girl I know who could make a guy in a funky old tux look good. Sabrina, you're the best."

She smiled. "Well, I figured that if you had to go retro, the least I could do was match you." She tapped her ears with her fingers. "Down to the last detail."

Harvey snorted in amusement. "Little smiley face earrings!"

"To match that awful smiley face stitched on your jacket."

Harvey blushed. "I hate to say it, but I didn't think you'd have the nerve to be seen with me in this suit, let alone match me." He suddenly remembered the corsage. "Oh, here. This is for you." As he helped her pin it on, he noticed something sparkle near the floor. "Uh, Sabrina, I think your shoes are glowing."

The fact was, Sabrina's shoes *were* glowing. In honor of Hilda, she'd taken the golden sandals from Hilda's shopping session and had Drest dye them light blue mixed with magical glitter dust. "Glad you like them," she said. "They're, uh . . . family heirlooms."

Now Harvey looked up and noticed something else. "What's that in your hair, a bow tie? I like it. Weird but cool."

It was indeed a bow tie. In honor of Zelda, Sabrina had taken the bow tie from Zelda's shopping session and dyed it to match her dress. For a final touch, she'd then trimmed it with dark blue satin. "I'm hoping to start a new fashion rage," she told Harvey, eating up his compliments. "So, Mr. Kinkle"—she held out her hand—"shall we be off to the ball?"

Harvey couldn't help but notice the nail polish on her proffered hand. "Hey, your fingernails just changed from blue to red! How'd they do that?"

"Magic," Sabrina answered, stifling a grin. *Ooo, red is for love! Aunt Vesta was right: it's fun to know how the people around you feel!*

Like a man in a dream, Harvey took her hand, and they headed for his car, which was parked at the curb. "How does dinner at Chic Eats sound?"

Chic Eats was a little Italian diner, slightly tacky, with checkered tablecloths and loud waiters. It wasn't the kind of place most prom couples would choose for dinner, but it had a certain charm. And it had Harvey written all over it. "Great," said Sabrina. "Let's do it!"

As Harvey started up the car engine, Sabrina settled back in her seat, feeling good for the first time in a week. *All my problems have been solved,* she thought happily, looking forward to a dazzling night.

Zelda stood by the gymnasium door, trying to blend in with the decor. Obviously the spring prom theme was Camelot, though the decorations, enthusiastic as they were, had no basis whatsoever in historical fact. Zelda had visited Camelot, after all, and she knew from personal experience that no self-respecting dragon would have been caught dead holding an hors d'oeuvre tray.

She looked around, but couldn't spot Sabrina and Harvey. No doubt they were still at dinner, since the prom hadn't officially begun yet. The band was just tuning up, and couples were only starting to arrive.

Zelda didn't like being so sneaky, standing right by the door. She'd intended to honor her agreement with her sisters and stay away from the prom. But she had seen that mischievous glint in Vesta's eyes and knew her older sister would break her word. If there was one person Sabrina didn't need at her spring prom, it was Vesta. Zelda intended to keep an eye out for trouble.

"How nice to see you again, Zelda," said Mr. Kraft, approaching her and nodding in greeting. "I'm glad you could chaperon our little celebration."

"Actually, this reminds me of one of Art's dinner parties," Zelda replied, "except he had his own caterers and the lighting wasn't so good."

Mr. Kraft blinked. "Art? You mean King Arthur, as in Camelot?" He laughed. "Good one. Say"—he leaned in closer—"is your charming sister here, too, perchance?" Kraft had once had a crush on Hilda, though his pursuit of her had cooled over the last few weeks. Apparently he was ready to try again.

"I'm afraid she's . . . busy at home," Zelda informed him.

He actually pouted. "Rats. I was kind of hoping—" Kraft stopped himself midsentence. "What do you mean she's busy at home? She's right over there." His eyes bugged out. "And who in the world is that with her?"

Zelda turned to find Hilda standing beside a mannequin knight in shining armor. And on the other side of the knight stood Vesta! Zelda wasn't sure what surprised her more—her younger sister's impossible presence or her older sister's outlandish Arthurian costume. Unlike Hilda, who wore a cute skirt and jacket combo, Vesta had decked herself out in a long gown and veil that Guinevere herself would have envied.

Zelda hurried over to them, trailed by a curious Mr. Kraft. "What are you doing here?" Hilda was saying to Vesta.

"Me?" Vesta responded innocently. "What are *you* doing here? Aren't you supposed to be grounded?"

"I'm here because I knew you'd show up," Hilda said.

"And I'm here because I want to be," Vesta declared.

"Neither of you should be here!" Zelda interjected.

"Well, look who it is. Miss Goody Two-shoes," said Vesta. She batted exquisitely mascared lashes at Mr. Kraft. "Hi, handsome."

Kraft nearly melted. Then he shook himself back to his senses. "Hilda, may I talk to you?"

Zelda grabbed Hilda's arm. "I get her first." Pulling her to one side, Zelda whispered, "Enough about why you're here—*how* are you here? You're supposed to be at home!"

"I realized that an It's-Just-Like-Being-There spell would let me leave the house," Hilda explained.

Zelda gasped. An It's-Just-Like-Being-There spell created a reflected image of the caster that duplicated whatever the caster did, but in a different location. That meant that a reflection of Hilda was at home now, going through the motions of what the real Hilda was doing. Their father's grounding spell was being fooled into thinking Hilda was really at home. "You're taking an awfully big risk," Zelda warned. "If the grounding spell detects the deception—"

"I'm doing this for Sabrina," said Hilda. "I knew Vesta would show up, and I was right—see?"

"I knew it, too, but I can handle her alone."

"No, you can't. Nobody can handle her."

"Well, my handling her alone is better than your being here against our father's orders!"

"Look, Sabrina is my responsibility too!"

Vesta glided between them. "Tut-tut, sisters, let's not argue."

"You stay out of this!" Zelda and Hilda both snapped.

All three sisters started to argue. Overwhelmed, Mr. Kraft waved his arms for attention. "Ladies, ladies, calm down! Whatever the problem is . . ." He paused as a strangely warm breeze whooshed past, mussing his hair. Hilda and Zelda stopped arguing, and Vesta looked at them in confusion. Kraft blinked as if waking from a dream, then tidied his hair. "Whatever the problem is," he repeated slowly, "I'm sure we can come to an amicable agreement. After all, it's only fair . . ."

The prom wasn't in full swing yet. Only half the couples had arrived, and the band had just begun to play. But Libby Chessler was already at work on the social scene, making sure that everyone was in the proper place, talking to the proper people, eating the proper food, and dancing in the proper spot. "Gordie," she said, tapping the geek on his shoulder. "You can't dance here."

Gordie and his date, a mousy girl named Paula, went pale. "We can't? Why not?"

Libby pointed at the floor. "See this design? You're not even inside the Round Table." She gently pushed them to the middle zone. "You'll have more room over here, closer to the band."

The two geeks grinned. "Gee, Libby, thanks!"

Libby smiled back. "It's only fair."

A warm breeze whooshed past Libby's date, Desmond Jacobi, ruffling his jacket. He absently buttoned it, saying to Libby, "Why do the teachers and parents have to stand around and chaperon all night? Shouldn't they get a chance to dance?"

Libby patted his arm. "Desmond, that's a wonderful idea. You and the other football players can take the chaperons' places so they can have some fun, too. It's only fair."

"Great!" Desmond went to round up his comrades.

Jill surveyed the food tables as her dress rustled in the warm breeze. "The freaks are all congregating at that back table," she noted. "All they're getting is fruit punch. Shouldn't they get some of the soft drinks, too?"

"Fix it," Libby ordered. "And make sure the other table supplies are distributed evenly." As Jill moved to obey, Libby saw Valerie and her date, Todd Earling, arrive. Hurrying over to them, she said, "Perfect! You're just in time!"

Valerie shied back. "For what?"

"To get your picture taken," Libby said, guiding them to the photo area. She forcibly maneuvered Valerie in front of the castle court backdrop. "This is the best one," she said. "Come on, Todd, the photographer hasn't got all evening."

As the photographer set up his camera, Todd took his place next to Valerie. "Cool. I thought we'd have to stand in front of that peasant hut backdrop, or maybe the kitchen one."

"Puh-lease," said Libby. "I'm having those atrocities removed. It's only fair that everyone get the best prom picture possible, right?"

Valerie shrugged. "Right!"

"Okay, Mr. Wolfman, you may begin," Libby said to the photographer. Then she rushed off to find Mr. Kraft. "Money, money, I need money," she muttered to herself. "Taking photographs is hard work. Mr. Wolfman definitely deserves more for this job." She barely felt the warm wind as it blew past, tickling the skin at the back of her neck. She was used to it by now.

Sabrina and Harvey finished dinner at Chic Eats and decided to take a leisurely moonlight drive before going to the prom. As Harvey put it, "I hate showing up first at parties. There's nobody to hide behind." They blared the radio for a while and had great fun trying to hold a coherent conversation over all the noise, then they stopped off at the Slicery for a game of Foosball in their prom outfits, just to wow the customers. Finally they headed for the big event.

They arrived at the Westbridge High School gymnasium to find a line of cheerleaders at the door. "Oh, great," said Sabrina. "The social gestapo is already on post to keep out the riff-raff."

"Are we riffraff?" Harvey asked.

"Let's find out."

They approached the door only to find the cheerleaders giving everyone who entered a piece of paper. "What's this?" Sabrina asked.

Cee Cee held one out to Sabrina. "It's a ballot, so you can vote for the best dance couple. Observe the dancers, and write down your choice. But you'd better hurry, it's almost time."

Sabrina accepted the paper. "Cool! What a great idea."

Cee Cee looked smug. "It was my idea. After all, it's only fair."

Sabrina's heart thumped. *"What* did you say?"

"I said, it's only fair."

"Hey, Sabrina, you feel okay?" Harvey asked her, noticing how the color was draining from her face.

She grabbed his arm. "C'mon, Harvey, we've got to get in there!"

Chapter 16

All the anxiety that had drained from Sabrina earlier that evening came rushing back when she entered the gym. The spring prom was in full swing, but Sabrina alone could see the events through a roiling yellow-and-purple haze. *The Fair Wind is back!* she thought in panic. *It's condensed into a fog and settled over everything!*

Teachers and parents were dancing up a storm while student chaperons stood watch by the doors. Several popular girls were standing alone against the wall, desperate for dance partners, while throngs of nerdish girls were fighting for the chance to dance with Gordie. The photographer was busily taking pictures of himself, and in the midst of all this, Libby was literally shoving food into geeks' hands, saying, "Eat this; it's really expensive!"

Sabrina knew things had gone too far when she caught Mrs. Quick taking donations for the dance band. "They're playing so well," the teacher said, "it's only fair that we buy them a yacht, don't you think?"

Trudy walked up to Sabrina and Harvey, her dance ballot in her hands. "Wow, you guys aren't even moving," she exclaimed. "I'm voting for you!"

Sabrina gathered her wits and tried to think of a solution. "Things aren't that bad yet," she said to herself. "Maybe I can fix them." And that's when she spotted Zelda in the crowd, dancing. "Omigosh, it's Aunt Zelda! Harvey, I'll be right back."

"Sure thing," Harvey said, and cut in front of a first-string football player. "Hey, man, lemme dance with your girlfriend."

The jock merely nodded, not the slightest bit upset. "Sounds fair," he said, and backed away.

Sabrina pushed her way through the throng of dancing bodies to discover her aunt Zelda dancing with Desmond Jacobi. "Hello, Sabrina," Zelda said cheerfully. "Isn't Des a cutey? He's been chaperoning so hard I thought he should get a chance to dance."

"What are you doing here?" Sabrina demanded. "You promised you wouldn't interfere anymore!"

Zelda twirled around, laughing. "I'm having a good time. Isn't it fair that I get to have fun on a Saturday night, too?"

"Oh, no," Sabrina said, "you've been affected!"

"Affected? Whatever do you mean?"

"Never mind." She looked around and spotted her aunt Hilda—dancing with Mr. Kraft! "Oh, great—two problems rolled into one." She hurried over. "Aunt Hilda, you're not supposed to leave the house!"

"And that is so not fair," Hilda responded. "I just had to come to your prom, so I used magic to fool Daddy's spell."

Mr. Kraft paused from dancing the Swim to take Hilda's hand and kiss it. "She used magic," he repeated cheerfully. "Hey, why can't we all use magic?"

"Yeah!" agreed Hilda. "Everybody should have magic. It's only fair!" She started to point her finger, but Sabrina grabbed it.

"Oh, no, you don't!" As Hilda frowned, Sabrina hastily added, "Uh, it'll be better if you wait till everybody gets here first."

Hilda thought about it. "Good idea. Okay."

Sabrina barely had time to sigh in relief before the song ended and a sultry voice said over the microphone, "Good evening, everyone, and welcome to the Westbridge High School spring prom. I'm Vesta, and I'll be hosting the selection of the king and queen. But first I'd like to announce the winners of the dance contest."

Sabrina ran up to the stage. "Aunt Vesta? What are you doing?"

Vesta leaned over, covering the microphone

with her hand. "Sabrina, you never told me you made a Fair Wind potion. Naughty girl."

"You—you can tell? Aren't you affected by it?"

"Of course not," said Vesta. "I wear Spell-Repel, the new nonstick formula that rolls on dry, doesn't stain delicate fabrics, and repels even the nastiest spell. I'm not fool enough to fall prey to any old spell that gets zapped my way, you know." She patted Sabrina on the head. "Now excuse me. I'm having far too much fun." Straightening up, she said into the microphone, "Ballots for the dance contest have been counted, and the winners are . . ." Cee Cee scurried across the stage and handed Vesta a paper. Vesta opened and read it. "I don't believe it. The winners are Sabrina Spellman and Harvey Kinkle!"

The crowd clapped, and Harvey was pushed forward to join Sabrina by the stage. "But we haven't even danced yet," Sabrina tried to tell them.

"Exactly," Vesta said, amused. "So it's only fair that you should win."

"That doesn't make any sense."

Handing Sabrina a trophy, Vesta remarked, "You're the one who tried to augment a Fair Wind potion, darling."

"Oh, this is all wrong!" Sabrina said desperately. "Aunt Vesta, won't you help me?"

"Before we choose the prom king and queen?" Vesta asked, shocked. "Certainly not." Raising the microphone to her lips, she announced, "And now for the moment you've all been waiting for. I give you this year's candidates for prom king!"

The candidates turned out to be Desmond Jacobi, Gordie, and one of the caterers. By unanimous applause, the caterer won. "But he's not even a student," Sabrina complained. Before anyone could say it, she said it herself: "I know, I know, that's what makes it fair." She ran back over to Zelda and Hilda, who were at the dessert table with Mr. Kraft, stuffing their faces with cookies. "Aunt Hilda, Aunt Zelda, can't you help me stop this, *please?*"

"Stop it?" Zelda asked, chewing a mouthful of carrot cake. "Are you kidding? This is wonderful!"

Hilda grabbed up a handful of chocolate-chip cookies. "How often can adults eat this much sugar without shame? It's only fair we get a chance to be pigs in public like kids are." And she shoveled them all in her mouth.

Mr. Kraft laughed. "Hilda, you look so cute with your cheeks bulged out like a squirrel's."

Sabrina slapped her hand to her forehead. "I can't take much more of this . . ."

She didn't have to, at least, not from her aunts. With a flash of magical light, Hilda suddenly started to fade. "Oh, no! Daddy's spell found me!"

Poof! She was gone.

Another flash of light and Zelda started to fade. "I'm caught in it, too! This isn't fair!"

Poof! She was gone.

Another flash and Mr. Kraft started to fade. "I have no idea what's going on, but I guess it's fair," he said, puzzled.

Poof! he was gone.

Up on the stage, Vesta finished announcing the candidates for prom queen. Libby, Trudy, and Valerie stood on the stage. "Everyone in favor of Libby?" Vesta said into her microphone.

Scattered clapping filled the air.

"Those in favor of Trudy?"

More scattered clapping.

"Those in favor of Valerie?"

The gym practically exploded with applause.

"Me?" Valerie shrieked in amazement. "I'm the *prom queen?*"

Vesta set the official prom queen tiara on Valerie's head. "Looks like it, darling. Judging by circumstances, you won because you'd normally never stand a chance, even over this pathetic little creature over here." Vesta gestured at Trudy. "Savor the moment. It's not likely ever to happen to you again."

Valerie could hardly move. The caterer who wore the prom king crown stepped to her side and took her arm. Highly entertained by it all, Vesta gave Valerie the microphone. "Speech, darling. Your public awaits."

Taking the microphone, Valerie gulped and stammered, "I, uh . . . I'm so honored . . ."

Everybody clapped.

"But I can't accept this. In all fairness, Libby should be prom queen. After all, she's popular and I'm not." Valerie took off her tiara and tried to give it to Libby, but Libby refused it.

"No way, Valerie, that wouldn't be fair," Libby said. "If anybody should win, it should be Trudy. You're both unpopular, but she's ugly, to boot."

Valerie nodded. "How incredibly right you are, Libby."

Trudy refused the tiara, too. "No, Valerie, you won it fair and square. It shouldn't matter that I'm uglier than you are—you're wimpier than I am."

The girls launched into an argument about why each *shouldn't* be prom queen, and when the argument threatened to become a free-for-all, Sabrina's patience reached its limit. With a wave of her finger, she chanted,

I've been wrong, I now confess.
To let me solve it, freeze this mess!

Everyone and everything froze, except for Vesta. *Must be the Spell-Repel,* Sabrina thought as her eldest aunt calmly zapped herself off the stage and over to Sabrina's side. "Excellent time freeze," Vesta complimented her. "Yet I sense it means only that you want help to make things right and you won't take no for an answer, correct?"

"Bingo."

With a put-upon expression, Vesta held up her hands. "Far be it from me to solve your problems for you, so I'll only give you a hint." She pointed straight up and a lightning bolt of golden witch magic hit the ceiling.

Chapter 17

☆

Sabrina looked up at a new fixture in the ceiling. "A fan? Aunt Vesta, I already tried that. It didn't work."

"Let me guess," Vesta said. "You tried to blow the Fair Wind away." When Sabrina nodded, Vesta continued, "You probably noticed that it eluded you. Most Fair Winds have a mind of their own. After all, it's only fair that they should."

"This is no time for jokes."

"I'm not joking. You pushed your Fair Wind away, so naturally, it retaliated. Now it won't listen to you at all. You've got to take control of it again."

"But how?" Then a little idea bell went *ping!* in Sabrina's head. "That's it! I need to reverse the fan and suck the Fair Wind *in!*"

Vesta gave her niece a hug. "Genius runs in our family."

Sabrina wasn't finished yet. "But I can do even better than that. If I turn the fan up high enough, I should be able to create a total social vacuum and reestablish the status quo, shouldn't I?"

Vesta regarded her niece with admiration. "Well, well, aren't we a clever little witch? Even I didn't think of that."

Focused on a plan of action now, Sabrina pointed at the fan that Vesta had created and magically enlarged it. When it was nearly half the size of the gym ceiling, she pointed again and zapped it on. As the blades began to turn, she felt a gentle upward tug.

"I suggest you eliminate the freeze spell," Vesta whispered in her ear, "or even a fan the size of Yankee Stadium won't have any effect."

"Good idea." Sabrina waved her finger over the prom crowd, chanting:

Everybody, back in motion
So I can stop my Fair Wind potion!

The ruckus on the stage instantly resumed. In an irrational rage, Libby, Valerie, and Trudy leaped at each other and began a ridiculous slapping fight as the prom crowd cheered them on. "Oh, dear," Sabrina said, "this isn't good." Thinking quickly, she pointed at the band. Immediately they began to play a slow love song, and when Sabrina pointed again, everybody in the crowd found a partner and began to dance.

"Sabrina?" came Harvey's voice. He reached out a hand to her. "Wanna danoc?"

She took his hand. "I'd love to."

As Sabrina, Harvey, and the rest of the dancers swayed to the music, the ceiling fan picked up speed. It pulled at the yellow-and-purple haze of the Fair Wind, which fled into a corner and tried to coalesce. The fan pulled harder and—with an audible *floop!*—sucked the Fair Wind up.

Then, slowly, the dancers rose up off the floor, hair flying in the fan's wind, clothes flapping, but no one seemed to notice, least of all Sabrina. She and Harvey just gazed at each other as they rose higher and higher. In minutes the floor was bare and the gymnasium was filled with people literally dancing on air in a perfect social vacuum.

If it had been up to Sabrina, she would have let the prom stay airborne. It was terribly romantic. But she knew it couldn't last. So with a flick of her finger, she slowed the fan back down. Gradually everyone sank to the floor in their correct social order: the nerds and geeks first, then teachers, then parents, then the athletes, and finally the cheerleaders.

When the song ended, silence claimed the gym. Everybody looked at everybody else. Mutters of "What happened?" and "I feel weird" touched Sabrina's ears, but she ignored them. All she saw was Harvey, who was smiling at her.

"Great dance," he said.

"Yeah," she answered.

Vesta broke the spell. "Congratulations, Sabrina," she said, making her way through the crowd.

Only then did Sabrina realize that Vesta had remained unaffected by the fan. Her aunt's hairstyle had remained unmussed, her Guinevere gown perfectly in order. Leaving Harvey for a moment, she joined her aunt. "You and that Spell-Repel," she commented.

"Hardly," Vesta replied. "Spell-Repel isn't that strong. No, I'm naturally immune to social vacuums. I'm simply too far above the mortal social structure."

"Uh-huh." Sabrina said no more about it. What worried her now was the prom itself. Although the partygoers did not clearly remember getting swept off their feet, they couldn't ignore their mussed hair and clothes. The prom would be doomed in the midst of such a mystery.

"Oh, for heaven's sake, don't look so stricken," Vesta told Sabrina. "I have just the thing to save the evening." She pointed her finger in a quick circle, and an arrow of golden witch magic sped once around the gym. The air of uncertainty that Sabrina had felt was gone, and everyone began laughing and joking as if nothing had happened.

"What did you do?" asked Sabrina warily.

"Nothing that your silly mortal friends wouldn't have done for themselves, if events had remained on a mortal track," claimed Vesta. "I just cast one of my Happy Ending spells. I use them all the time. How do you think I live such a perfect life? Now no matter what else happens, everyone will go home thinking the prom was the best ever. Satisfied?"

Sabrina hugged her aunt. "Yes. Thanks . . . for everything."

Vesta flashed her radiant smile. "You're welcome. Just don't tell Zelda or Hilda that I helped out. I've cultivated a contrary image for so many years that it would be a shame to ruin it now." Taking Sabrina by the shoulders, she physically turned her around. "Now go back to your Harvey fellow. He's waiting."

When Sabrina glanced back over her shoulder, Vesta was gone.

By the time Sabrina got home, she had totally forgotten that Zelda and Hilda had been at the prom. She'd also forgotten that Mr. Kraft had disappeared with them. She entered the house to hear the three of them arguing in the kitchen.

"What am I doing here?" Kraft was saying.

"Hey, don't look at me," came Hilda's voice. "I had absolutely nothing to do with it."

"Stop it, both of you," Zelda said. "It can't be helped."

Oh, great, Sabrina thought. *Aunt Hilda's grounding spell pulled all three of them back here and now Mr. Kraft is wigging out. This is all my fault!* She considered tiptoeing up the steps and hiding in her room, but that would only prolong the agony. *I might as well get this over with.*

Hesitantly she opened the kitchen door and peeked inside. "Hi, I'm home?"

Zelda, Hilda, and Mr. Kraft were sitting at the kitchen table playing Monopoly. "Oh, hi, Sabrina," said Hilda. "How'd your evening go?"

"Uhh . . ." Sabrina wasn't sure what to say, what with Kraft sitting right there. "Good?" she ventured.

"Excuse me," Zelda told her fellow players, and got up from her chair. She gestured Sabrina into the living room as Kraft said to Hilda, "Just because I rolled a six, I have to go to jail? That's not fair!"

"I didn't make up the rules," Hilda answered.

Zelda took Sabrina to the far end of the living room before speaking. "We know what happened tonight," she said in a low voice. "This came in the toaster a few minutes ago." She held out a card from Vesta, which read simply, "Happy Ending!" Zelda continued, "The moment we opened it, a Happy Ending spell hit Mr. Kraft. Now he thinks he's here with us because the prom was boring."

Sabrina sighed with relief. "Oh, good."

"No, not so good—at least, not for you," Zelda said sternly. "You've got some explaining to do tomorrow about a certain Fair Wind potion."

"Okay, okay," said Sabrina. "Guilty as charged."

Zelda's stern expression melted away. "But don't worry. You can explain at the movies with Hilda and me."

Sabrina did a double take. "Huh?"

"It's the least we can do, considering what we put you through." She studied Sabrina's dress. "I like the way you solved the problem of the dress."

Sabrina smiled. "Well, in the end, I decided to wear something from everybody. After all, it was only fair."

About the Authors

David Cody Weiss is in actuality a mad scientist who shocked the literary world when he invented the perfect writing android, which he affectionately named Bobbi JG Weiss. To David's surprise, man and machine fell in love and have since become the ultimate married couple—David tells Bobbi what to do, and Bobbi tells David to stick it in his ear. However, they do write great books together—for instance, the one in your hands right now. Among other books they've written are five more *Sabrina the Teenage Witch* books, three *Star Trek: Starfleet Academy* novels, a *Secret World of Alex Mack* novel, and three *Are You Afraid of the Dark?* novels. They have also written animation, many comic books, trading cards, Disney Online games, and even a trilogy of films that never got made.

David is currently inventing new modifications for Bobbi, one of which he hopes will allow Bobbi to plot, write, and get paid for novels at the speed of light. As for Bobbi, well, she's working on her own android—one that obeys without question.